RIPLEY

The Road to Acceptance

REBECCA ROBINSON

RIPLEY: The Road to Acceptance

Author photo taken by Gary Collier, Collier Photo: www.collierphoto.ca

ISBN: 978-1-77069-425-5

Printed in Canada.

Word Alive Press
131 Cordite Road, Winnipeg, MB R3W 1S1
www.wordalivepress.ca

WORD ALIVE PRESS
Just Write!

MIX
Paper from responsible sources
FSC® C016245

ALSO BY REBECCA ROBINSON

When Times Stands Still under the pen name of Rebecca Hickson (Xulon Press 2005)

ISBN 1-594677-27-1 Printed in the United States

The Narrow Road Series

Roseway – The Road that Never Ends (Word Alive Press 2012)

Ripley – The Road of Acceptance (Word Alive Press 2012)

Jenn – The Road of Sacrifice (Word Alive Press 2012)

Library and Archives Canada Cataloguing in Publication

Robinson, Rebecca Wills
Ripley : the road to acceptance / Rebecca Wills Robinson.

ISBN 978-1-77069-425-5

I. Title.

PS8635.O2635R56 2011 C813'.6 C2011-907663-2

Contents

Acknowledgements

To the love of my life, my wonderful husband Danny, I dedicate this entire series. The encouragement you have shown me many times motivated me to write. It was not that long ago I had to walk my own road to acceptance. The Lord brought you into my life and made my broken road straight again. Thank you for making me laugh along *The Narrow Road* and for helping me look beyond my own limited vision to find the joy in each new day. Just as I have penned the fictional words in these stories, God has penned my life from beginning to end. I praise our Lord who truly saves us while working His mysterious plans by intertwining the roads in our lives.

I must acknowledge the inspiration of the Holy Spirit. I'd pray and the words would flow like a river. When I thought my storyline was crazy and far out there, God introduced me to two different ladies: Terry-Lynne and Sherrilyn. Both women had death experiences and crossed over to get a glimpse of the other side. Again, I must thank the courageous people who give their testimonies so others can see the healing power of Christ in their lives, the transforming power that changes lives from darkness to light.

Friends are like the water to a garden. I thank Sue Beadman and Anne Acacia for looking over my first drafts and helping me with some of the medical and legal terminology. Gwendolyn Elliot and Tom Buller, thank you for your detailed edits on each book and also for your constructive critique which I believe will help me to become an even better writer. Your motivating comments may result in yet another series of books.

1
Unleashed Imagination

Camay took a sip of her tea as she sat on her new deck, a renovated schoolhouse built in 1910 which was now her new home. It was called the School of Zion. It only seemed fitting that she would open her laptop and sit down to write a book. It was, after all, an old grey brick schoolhouse.

Once was the day when little children ran up the front steps as the school bell rang from the belfry. The belfry was now somewhat bare. The wood looked old, ready to collapse should a strong wind blow. One could hear the song of the doves which made the belfry their permanent home. Yes, one could picture the children laughing, yelling, and screaming as young school children do. It wasn't hard to imagine classes being taught and the children sitting at old wooden desks.

That was not the story she was going to write today.

Camay looked at the blank pages and saw her reflection in the screen on her laptop. She smiled back at herself. The mood was set with water running into her ceramic water fountain. The dog was lying in the grass, birds were chirping, an owl was hooting in the distance, and the majestic mountains surrounded her.

She began to get into her writing zone, typing a few words. The keys clicked. She smiled at herself again, quite pleased as she looked at her reflection once more. Wearing a lovely straw hat with a yellow scarf tied around the brim, it hung lazily down her back, mingling with her curly brown hair. Wearing her designer glasses she imagined herself to be somewhat like the famous author Lucy Maude Montgomery, in her younger days as an aspiring writer. If only she could write a good book like *Anne of Green Gables*.

Camay was in her mid-forties and wanted to be a successful writer. She had only written one book, but it was her passion and God's calling that motivated her to write.

Her memory slipped her back in time, to two years earlier, remembering what should have been one of the happiest days of her life, the long awaited arrival of her first published book. Years of writing and editing, tears and prayers had gone into the making of that book. Surely she had gone out with her husband, Skylor, to celebrate with close friends.

They made dinner reservations at the Villa Rocello restaurant. Champagne was on ice. Camay was dressed to the nines. Her brown hair flowed down over her shoulders, enhancing the sparkles within her dark brown eyes. Camay was bubbling over with excitement as she waited with anticipation. She couldn't keep this to herself any longer.

Picking up the phone, she dialled her mother's number.

"Mother, guess what? My book's arrived today. You should see it. The cover looks amazing. I'm so excited."

Her mother joined with her in excitement. "That is great news, honey. I know you have waited a long time for this moment. I'm so happy for you. Is Skylor home yet? What did he say?"

"No, he's not home yet. He's late again. He knows we're going out for dinner with Jack and Marie." Disappointment began to edge into her voice. "Actually, I'm going to phone him at work again and see what is taking him so long. I called a couple times already. He told me he was going to work out at the gym after work. But when I phoned the recreation center, they said he wasn't there. He just never seems to be here when I need him. There is always some excuse, and I have found the excuses don't always match. I'll talk to you later. I'll see if I can track him down."

"Okay honey. Talk to you later."

Camay snapped back to the present time where she now lived alone in the schoolhouse. Skylor and she had been together for twenty-five years. He'd had an affair with another woman. Perhaps it had been a mid-life crisis that led him to find happiness elsewhere.

They had three children together. Camay had stayed home and taken care of the children and the house all those years. When her marriage broke up, the children headed off to college and out on their own. She managed to get a job working for a fast-paced advertising company where she had worked for two years. This kept her very busy—too busy. After enduring the pinch of time, she decided to take the chance of working part-time, giving her time to write and follow her dreams.

Today was her first day off from work. She had jumped ship, escaped the trap—the cave of the working world. Though her heart was willing, the block monster was always ready to put negative messages into her mind and stop her flow of words. *Who considers writing books to be a job? Isn't it just a hobby? What will you write that could possibly interest anyone?*

She pushed those thoughts away and pressed forward as if to convince herself otherwise. *It doesn't really matter,* she thought. *What matters is that I love to write. Now I will have the time to write.*

Looking at her reflection as she typed her page, her imagination became sidetracked again. *I look like someone out of a movie, with my blue-framed glasses and straw hat. Oh well, if that is what it takes to get some inspiration, I'll wear this hat.*

She swatted a mosquito and leaned in to type.

The phone rang.

"Oh, hi. It's me, Amanda, from work. The coffee machine is broken. Who do I call to fix it?"

It was nice to be needed. It gave her a sense of importance, knowing that she had not been replaced at work yet. She may have been sitting on her deck, but in her mind she was thinking about work. Had she made the right decision? Still, she felt peace and a sense of freedom which compelled her to want to explode with words of her unleashed imagination.

Once again, Camay stared at the page, wondering what to write.

In deep thought, she was suddenly startled by a "Hello."

Camay jumped out of her seat, almost spilling her tea off the table. While Camay had been focused on the empty page in front of her, a woman had walked right up to her deck.

"Oh my goodness, you startled me," Camay said.

"I'm sorry," the woman said. "My name is Roseway. I will be your neighbour in a couple of months. My fiancé Joseph and I will be moving in permanently after the wedding. I was just over at the farm fixing up a few things, and I don't have the proper tools, so I thought I would introduce myself to you and also see if you had some tools I could borrow."

With an inquisitive smile, Camay asked, "Where did you say your place is?"

"We rented the McKinney farm. It is about a quarter mile down the road."

"Oh yes, they have a nice piece of property. I imagine you will be quite busy fixing up that place."

"Yeah, we have a lot of work to do. I plan on planting a vegetable garden. We also got a deal on some livestock. I'll do most of the farming while Joseph continues to drive the transport."

"You seem familiar to me," Camay said with a curious expression. "Have we met before? My name is Camay."

"No, I don't think so. I only returned to Kelowna three years ago. I've been living with my mother, brother, and sister ever since. My mother, Noreen, works at the diner."

"Is your mother Noreen Shafer?"

"Yes, that is correct."

"That's where I know you from. You are the young girl who was kidnapped from that awful man, Joe Demerse. I remember you from the news. It was just around the time that I moved here from Ontario. When I saw your story on the news, I remember thinking how nice it was to hear that your story had a happy ending. The news is so depressing most of the time."

"Yes, I suppose you are right," Roseway said. "I don't watch much television at all. It's a waste of time, if you ask me. Do you happen to have any tools I could borrow? I need a couple screwdrivers and a hammer."

"Come on over to my shed and we will have a look."

They walked along the path. A variety of wild flowers and tall grass brushed against their legs as they walked. The majestic white-capped mountains loomed in the distance like giant statues. The shed was covered in barn boards.

Camay opened the wooden hinge doors. Inside was a variety of tools.

"This shed is my toolbox," Camay said. "Help yourself to whatever you need. Please, just put everything back in its place when you are finished with them."

"Wow! That is very kind of you. Much appreciated. Thank you."

"Not a problem, Roseway. Guess I better get back to writing. We will have to get together for tea, perhaps when you get settled into the old farm. If you need any help, just let me know."

"Thanks again, Camay. I'll be sure to visit."

2
Wedding Day

The church doors opened wide. Joseph and Roseway stood under the mistletoe. Their lips met as cameras flashed. Snowflakes fell from the sky like confetti. Friends and family gathered around them, smiling. Some exchanged pleasant conversation. It was an old, eighteenth-century church with big oak doors, wooden oak benches and stained glass windows. Outside, parked in front of the church, were two white draft horses bridled in decorative harnesses, ready to pull the red sleigh that was covered with holly.

Rose was wearing a simple, white, long-sleeved dress intricately knit from lamb's wool. She looked like a princess with her mahogany hair up off her face, showing her delicate features. Joseph's brown eyes sparkled like a deer caught in headlights as he looked into her eyes. His tanned face and black hair brought out his handsome demeanour. He was dressed in a white suite with a holly berry red shirt that complemented Rose's flowered bouquet of roses and baby's breath. He whisked her up into his strong arms and carried her to the coach. The driver of the coach pulled on the reins and nudged the horses to walk forward.

Friends and family followed the short distance to the reception hall at Big White resort, nestled in the mountains. It was just a small town hall that was nicely decorated. A banquet table was lavished with fine homemade salads, lovely garnishes and bowls filled with sherbet punch and floating strawberries. Everyone danced to the local fiddle players as that ole mountain music played on into the night. Giddy laughter and pleasant conversation set the hall abuzz.

It was time for the dance of the bride and the groom. The band softly played the song *From This Moment* as Rose's dearest friend, Ripley, sang. Her voice was angelic. Everyone gathered around Rose and Joseph and watched the two of them lost in each other's arms. Rose clumsily stumbled a couple times over Joseph's big feet, but barely even noticed. With her arms wrapped around his neck, her starry eyes glazed over as she looked into his. He held her close and frequently kissed her cheeks, oblivious to the spectators watching. The kisses sent warmth through her body as if they were their very first kisses.

They both had remained chaste throughout their two-year engagement. Roseway was now twenty years old. In worldly wisdom she was still naive, vulnerable and in some ways had a childlike innocence. Joseph was a mature twenty-seven, but at the same time he was like a teenager in love for the first time. A longing to be together physically for the very first time made their hearts beat as one. Their kisses were electric. Feeling each other's bodies close together as they danced perked the river of love and attraction within them like a hunger needing to be fed. Just as the song ended, he lavished her with a kiss that made her knees feel weak. His soft lips melted on hers like strawberries dipped in chocolate. The song ended and friends and family clapped to cheer them on.

The partying continued into the early hours of the morning. Joseph and Rose couldn't take their eyes off of each other all through the night. Ripley sat leaning against the wall most of the night. Ever since she had banged her head when Big Joe Demerse pushed her, she had suffered reoccurring headaches whenever she was stressed. Ripley looked stunning in her royal blue dress with her blond, shiny hair hanging down over her shoulders. She was alone at the wedding, as her boyfriend JD was teaching seminars at the university.

How Ripley wished that JD could have been there with her. Classes and seminars in psychology often kept him away from attending special events. Standing against the wall watching Roseway and Joseph made her reminisce over the last three years since she had first met Roseway. In that short time, they had all changed in so many ways. Joseph worked hard to prepare financially for their future. Roseway had time to reconnect with her brother Billy, her sister Sue, and her mother Noreen. Ripley was ready to settle down and marry JD, and perhaps start a family. What concerned Ripley was wondering if Roseway was ready for marriage. To Ripley, Roseway still seemed too young and naive to know what life was really all about. She was so sheltered, after living with Big Joe in the wilderness all those years.

When Ripley saw Joseph standing alone, she quickly grabbed him by the arm and asked him if she could have this dance. Rose was dancing with her brother Billy. Joseph accepted the dance, while complimenting her on the great job she did singing.

"Ripley, I didn't know you could sing. You did a terrific job."

"Well, thank you, Joseph. It was the least I could do, since you are marrying my best friend." Feeling protectiveness toward Roseway, she added, "However, I hope you know what you are doing."

Perplexed, Joseph asked, "What do you mean?"

Ripley grinned as she spoke with concern. "I hope Roseway is ready for marriage. With all she has been through, and there are so many adjustments she has had to make already. Now she is getting married. I just hope she is mature enough to take on the role of wife, while still taking botany classes and taking care of that big farm. I guess what I want to say to you, Joseph, is that you better take good care of her or you'll have me to contend with." She grinned with a subtle yet serious expression behind her smile.

Joseph knew how much Ripley loved and cared for Roseway. It was a strong bond they shared. At times it seemed as strong as the bond Joseph shared with Roseway. He reassured Ripley. "You don't have to worry, Ripley. I love her very much, and I'll take good care of her."

Ripley put her hand on the side of her head and winced with pain, but she continued to speak. "I can see that you love her." The pain stabbed into her head like a machete.

Joseph lowered his eyebrows as he observed her. "What is the matter? You look pale as a ghost."

She leaned her head on Joseph's shoulder, grimacing with the pain. "Actually, I don't feel all that well."

Jokingly, Joseph asked, "Too much to drink?"

Ripley didn't recognize the joke. "I don't drink," she snapped as the pain increased. "Why would you say a dumb thing like that?" The pain intensified. "Ow!" Ripley rubbed her head through her blond hair.

Concerned, Joseph responded. "I didn't mean anything by it. What has gotten into you?"

Ripley was short-tempered, irritated by the pain. Behaving like a different person, she started slurring her words as if drunk. "Nothing has gotten into me. What are you accusing me of doing?"

"Chill out, Ripley. You are getting all worked up over nothing."

"Don't tell me to chill out. Nobody tells me what to do." Her thinking was confused. As if a machete was withdrawn from deep within her, a warm sensation flooded from the top of her head to the tips of her toes. "Oh, Joseph, I really don't feel good at all." Ripley held her head again as her legs buckled from under her. She fell onto Joseph. He caught her in his arms and realized that something was seriously wrong as she fell unconscious.

Joseph put his big arms around her, then gently laid her to the floor and yelled, "Someone call an ambulance! Ripley has passed out."

The music stopped and time stood still. Rose ran over to Ripley and Joseph.

"Oh my God, what has happened?"

Joseph looked bewildered. "I don't know. We were dancing and having a conversation and then she started acting weird. Next thing I knew she passed out in my arms. She was holding her head and she started slurring her words. I don't know, maybe she had a stroke or something?"

Roseway's brother Billy worked with the ski patrol team at Big White Resort and he had his first aid. He checked Ripley's vital signs and radioed for a chopper to take her to the hospital. It would take too long for an ambulance to drive up the mountain and back down. Billy didn't want to take the chance for severe brain damage to occur if it was indeed a stroke. A couple of medics tended to Ripley. The music stopped playing. The band leader asked everyone to take a seat while the medics did what they needed to do. Roseway was so worried about Ripley that she wanted to forget this was her wedding day. Roseway's mother Noreen quickly came and stood beside Roseway and put her arm around her. Joseph also stood beside her as the medics put Ripley on a stretcher. Billy volunteered to go with them in the chopper and give everyone an update on her condition when they reached the hospital.

Roseway spoke with determination. "I'm going with her."

Noreen tried to convince her to stay at the wedding. "Honey, this is your wedding day. Stay here. You can't do anything for Ripley. She would want you to stay and enjoy the rest of your special day."

"Mom, Ripley is my best friend. I have to be there with her."

"What about Joseph? He is your husband and he needs you, too."

Joseph looked speechless, then blurted out, "I'll come with you, darling."

Noreen opposed the idea. She knew how long they had both waited for this day to arrive and she didn't want anything to spoil it. "This is your honeymoon. Spend your first night together. Ripley wouldn't want it any other way. Billy will go with her now and I'll get a ride down shortly. I will call Ripley's mother. We will let you know her condition as soon as we find out anything from the doctors."

Billy yelled out, "The chopper is here and they have to take her. We don't have time to waste!"

The paramedics lifted the stretcher and Ripley started to have a seizure. Her body fought the restraints. They put the stretcher back down until the seizure seemed to cease. Quickly they picked up the stretcher and carried her out to the chopper. Roseway looked on, totally scared at what was happening to her friend.

With authority and control, Billy said to Roseway and Joseph, "Stay here, and I'll call you when we get to the hospital. Don't worry, Sis. Ripley will be fine. She is in good care."

Roseway stood biting her lip. Never had she felt so torn within herself. She wanted to go with Ripley, yet felt pressured to stay at the wedding even though all the excitement and joy she had been feeling quickly dwindled like a balloon whose air just emptied. The band began to play music again. Then they played the last dance.

Feeling like she was just going through the motions, Roseway felt more like a ragdoll being swept across the floor. *I should be with Ripley. Oh God, please let her be alright.*

Joseph held her close, sensing the separation. He could tell her mind was worrying about Ripley. His mind wondered, too. They said their goodbyes to all the well-wishers. Something seemed so amiss. Both Joseph and Rose waved goodbye with tears in their eyes as they looked back at everyone. The horse-drawn buggy was waiting outside to take them to their condominium at the lodge where they would spend the night. The night sky was dark. Stars lit the darkness like sparkling diamonds. A blue ring glowed around the full moon. Warm steam extruded from the horses' nostrils as they pulled the buggy forward. Joseph and Rose wrapped themselves in a warm blanket, cuddling close while looking at the stars.

Joseph lifted Roseway down from the buggy and carried her to the door. Roseway opened the door with one hand while her other arm wrapped around his neck. He carried her over to the bed covered in rose petals. He gently removed the wrap from her shoulders and kissed her cold cheeks. She brushed his black hair from his forehead while looking deep into his sparkling brown eyes. Rose half smiled with a disappointing grin and a tear in the corner of her eye. *I should be so happy at this moment. Instead I feel so sad and detached. Why do I feel so torn inside? I can't show it to Joseph. It would spoil this moment for him.*

Joseph sensed her hesitation and whispered, "Ripley is in good hands. Don't worry. We will go to the hospital in the morning. I love you, Rose."

Roseway loved him with everything she had in her. Joseph's heavy breath was sweet on her neck as he undid her wedding dress. Roseway blushed as she undid the snap buttons on his shirt one at a time. Her thoughts were spinning, thinking about Ripley while enjoying the pleasure of his touch. Guilt was hindering. She wanted to give Joseph the pleasure they both had waited to enjoy. Was Ripley going to be okay? Pictures of Ripley lying on the stretcher so still, so pale, invaded her mind. The pleasure of Joseph's touch pulled her thoughts back and forth. Joseph continued to take her breath away. His touch was passionate. Heat combed her body like a warm wave. His muscular arms seemed ever so appealing as he held himself up over top of her. They kissed a thousand kisses, loving each other with longed anticipation. Joseph was so gentle with her, as if she were a china doll. The hunger within them was quenched like a long burning fire. They then held on tight to each other, like Siamese twins with one heartbeat. Rose cried with an overwhelming feeling of release as she spoke the words, "I love you, too, Joseph."

Joseph looked at Roseway, wondering if he had hurt her. "Why are you crying? Are you alright? Did I hurt you?"

"No, you didn't hurt me. That was the most beautiful experience I've ever had. I've never felt as loved as you have just made me feel. I'm glad we waited until our wedding night. It just seems that much more special. How about you, what do you feel?"

"My darling, I am numb all over. The pleasure you have bestowed on me was incredible. I could make love to you all over again, and again, and again."

He nuzzled her neck again with more kisses. The phone rang. Roseway jumped up out of bed like the house was on fire. Joseph fell back in the bed with his hands on his head, feeling their loving moment snuffed out like a flickering candle.

"Hello, Roseway speaking."

"Hi Rose, it's me, Billy. The doctor is in with Ripley now. They are treating her at this time. Ripley is in a coma. They are taking x-rays and a brain scan as we speak, then they will be able to assess any damage. No one can go in to see her yet. I'll wait here until the doctors give some information."

"We will come to the hospital first thing in the morning," Roseway said. "See you then." She hung up the phone.

The interruption of the phone call had broken the romance. Joseph was trying not to show his disappointment and concern. His thoughts were eating away at him like a mouse on cheese. *Why did this have to happen to Ripley? Lord, we planned everything for this day, dreaming it would be perfect. We waited for this moment for such a long time, remaining pure before you. Now this unexpected event has turned everything upside down. Everything seems strained by the upheaval and interruptions. We are to leave tomorrow for our honeymoon. With this happening, I know Roseway won't want to go. I could never find my place in this bond of friendship that seems so exclusive to them only.*

Roseway interrupted Joseph's deep thought. "Honey, that was Billy. They have taken some tests. Could we go to the hospital in the morning? I'm worried sick about Ripley."

With a deep sigh Joseph answered, "I know you are worried. I am worried too, but we just got married. Couldn't we at least sleep in a little, maybe have a nice breakfast together and then go? By the sounds of it, Ripley is not coherent to even know if you are there or not."

"Okay Joseph, we will go after breakfast." Roseway wanted to make him happy. She felt the strain in his request, even though it seemed a little unsympathetic to how she was feeling. Her answer to Joseph put a little more spirit back into him. He kissed her again. They lavished their love on one another until they fell asleep.

Roseway felt so in love. The intimacy they enjoyed together was so real and powerful. She had never felt closer to anyone in her life as she did that morning. The sexual connection seemed to fill an emptiness she had always felt. The desire to be loved by her husband, a man, had been a hunger deep inside of her for a long time. Her entire life she had longed to feel a loving touch. From her father Big Joe, all she ever received was a backhand or a beating. She never knew how much the love of a man would mean to her heart and soul until that wedding night. Although there were distractions, worry and concern, Roseway knew she wanted more of his loving. It was like giving a candy to a child for the first time. After they made love, she could have laid in his arms all day. It felt safe, and warm—a feeling she had never felt to that extent. She thanked God for Joseph and for what they shared. Her only concern was Ripley's well-being. Ripley was her best friend, and they had been through so much together. They were friends who stuck closer than sisters.

The newlyweds had a romantic breakfast. Joseph surprised Roseway by ordering room service. The waiter brought them a plate of fresh fruit, along with a dish of pancakes, bacon and pure maple syrup. They fed each other strawberries, tickled each other under the blankets and laughed, enjoying the moment like a snapshot in a picture book.

Then it was getting late in the morning, and Roseway thought they had better prepare to go to the hospital.

3
Place of Many Mansions

Ripley lay in an unconscious state, oblivious to what the doctors were doing around her and to her. It was like she was caught in a new dimension. A white light shone through a long white tunnel. She walked cautiously. The silence was deafening. The light was so bright it made her squint. Her blond hair shined like golden silk. There was something peaceful about this tunnel.

As she walked into the tunnel, she began to hear the music of a harp. It was soft to the ears, a beautiful melody. At the end of the tunnel was a door sparkling with diamonds. Big stones mixed with little stones. The diamonds changed colours. These colours were heavenly like none she had ever seen. The light seemed to shine through them from the other side of the door. In amazement, she touched the door with her childlike fingertips. Suddenly, the door began to open. Standing in the doorway was a little angel with wings like that of a butterfly, adorned with many different colours. Her face was dainty, innocent and the colour of a pearl. Her voice was gentle in tone, much like the tiny little harp she held in her hand. The angel welcomed Ripley through the door.

"Please come in, Ripley, I've been expecting you," Spoke the angel with a calming, gentle voice.

Not realizing where she was or what had happened, Ripley felt mystified. "You have?"

"Yes, Ripley, my name is Acacia, like the acacia tree."

"It is nice to meet you, Acacia. Are you an angel? Am I dead?"

"Ripley, I am one of God's messenger angels, and no, you are not dead. You are very much alive."

"Why am I here?"

"God has brought you here for His great purpose. It would seem that God has a calling on your life. God is Holy and perfect, and because he is Holy, He is all knowing. God has sent me to help you on your journey."

"What journey am I going on?"

"Ripley, God has heard all your cries during your lifetime. He has been there with you between the porch and the altar, whether on your knees in prayer or on your way home. He knows your struggles, and the people who have hurt you. God knows the loneliness and the hunger you have experienced. Because God loves you and cares for you, He is going to send you on a journey to help you overcome these things that pull you in different directions and away from Him. God knows your heart. Some things can only be known from within. Other things are known by what we see, touch, smell, feel and experience.

"Do you want to overcome these things that often make you sad? You don't have to go on this journey. If you decide you would rather go back to the way things are, your wish will be granted. If you choose to trust God and take this journey, you must realize that it will be a difficult challenge with many demons to conquer and obstacles to overcome. God will only take you to these places by your own free will. What you will see and experience will utterly amaze you. Through this process, you will be changed to be more like Him."

After a moment of silence to ponder every word that Acacia had spoken, Ripley replied, "Yes, I want to go on this journey for God."

"Ripley, the first step you are going to take in this journey is called the road of acceptance. This road is a treacherous one with many curves, steep cliffs and detours. On this road you will learn how to first accept yourself the way God accepts you. When you can accept yourself, you will then learn to accept other people, good or bad. The bumpiest part of this road is accepting the things you cannot change, and learning how to change the things you can.

"Come with me, Ripley, and I will take you into the first room. Our father has prepared a place of many mansions. I will take you through only one mansion and through a couple of rooms. The rest of the rooms you will have to go alone. Are you ready?"

With some fear, Ripley took a deep breath and said, "Okay, let's go."

Acacia moved her wings up and down as she flew around Ripley. Dust fell from her wings onto Ripley. Ripley's clothing instantaneously changed. She was now wearing a yellow dress.

Ripley objected, "Do I have to wear this thing? I hate wearing dresses. They are so uncomfortable. Can't I wear blue jeans? This is not me. I look ugly in yellow. Why, look at my knobby knees. Yellow is such an ugly colour on me."

Acacia interrupted. "Are you quite finished complaining? Did you hear the things you just said about yourself?"

Ripley didn't realize how negative she was about herself until she thought about the words she had spoken.

Preparing Ripley to begin, Acacia informed her, "I want to show you something. This is a picture of what God witnessed when you were a little girl in the fifth grade."

With that, Acacia flapped her wings again and, as if transported into a time machine, Ripley found herself sitting on a school desk. She looked around the room and saw all the children from her fifth grade class. She smiled at the vision, excited to see her old classmates. There was Bobbie, he sat across from her. Susie, Cathy and Debbie each sat at their desks on either side of Ripley's desk that was in the middle. Ripley watched the class from the third person, the way God would watch and see everything that goes on.

Ripley noticed that she was wearing the same yellow dress that Acacia had placed on her. Ripley's expression began to change, remembering that day as she watched. Susie, Cathy, Debbie and Bobbie were laughing hysterically. Ripley watched herself start to cry as she got angry at her friends. The entire class was laughing at Ripley now, and pointing at her. They were chanting *knobby knees Ripley, knobby knees Ripley*. Ripley didn't think it was funny at all. Her feelings were so hurt and she felt so ugly and embarrassed that she ran out of the room. The vision of the classroom continued. Ripley watched what happened when she had left the room. She saw the teacher, Mrs. Latimer, yelling at the children to be quiet and sit in their seats.

"Who started this name-calling? I want to know right now or the entire class will stay for detention tonight and each night until I find out."

The class was silent for a moment. Little Nina put up her hand. "Mrs. Latimer, I started it." With that, the school bell rang and the class was over. Mrs. Latimer dismissed the class and told Nina to stay behind. The children all ran out of the room, free as birds.

With just Mrs Latimer and Nina in the room, Nina explained why she did what she did. "Ripley looked so pretty in her yellow dress that I was jealous. I always wished that I could wear a pretty dress. My mother never buys me dresses because she says that my legs are too ugly and a dress wouldn't look right with my artificial leg." Mrs. Latimer looked as Nina pulled up her pant leg to show her the prosthetic leg. "My mother told me that the other children would make fun of me. In my jealousy, I made fun of Ripley. Now I realize that I shouldn't have said to Susie and Debbie that Ripley had knobby knees. I don't even know what knobby knees look like. I'm sorry; I never realized that the entire class would tease Ripley. Her legs are normal."

Mrs. Latimer spoke in a soft tone. "Please come here, Nina."

Nina slowly walked to the front of the glass and stuck out her hands, waiting for Mrs. Latimer to hit them with the belt. She closed her eyes, waiting for the blow. Mrs. Latimer grabbed her little hands and pushed them down to her side. Bending down to Nina's height, she reached her arms around her and gave her a hug, saying, "Well Nina, I believe we have learned a valuable lesson today about name-calling and how our words can hurt others.

The vision ended and Ripley found herself back in the room in the mansion. With an embarrassing grin, she looked at Acacia. "I was in Nina's class two years in a row and I never knew she had an artificial leg. I feel like such a fool."

The little angel commented, "We never know the things that are hidden, do we?"

"All those years, I took what they said to me as the truth. For years, I thought my legs were funny-looking. I never put on a dress again until Roseway's wedding."

Acacia fluttered her wings and instantly Ripley was wearing a pair of jeans and a white collared shirt. "Well Ripley, are you ready to continue to go further down the road to acceptance?"

4
The Dark Room

Ripley took a deep breath and replied with a "Yes." Another door opened, and darkness entered the room. Ripley stood in the entranceway that lead into the next room. It seemed dark like a dungeon. There was nothing beautiful or inviting about this room. It made Ripley feel very uncomfortable. It had an eeriness about it.

Hesitantly, Ripley walked through the door. With a slam, the door closed behind her. Now the only light in the room was the light from Acacia's eyes and the glimmer from her wings. Goosebumps crawled on Ripley's arms like a colony of ants on her skin, making the hairs on her arm stand to attention like soldiers. Fear embraced her, not knowing what she would find in the darkness.

Acacia said to Ripley, "You will have to experience this room on your own. I have been instructed to leave. I will see you again soon."

Ripley objected. "No, please don't go. I am afraid of the dark. Do I have to be here alone?"

"Remember, Ripley, the last lesson learned. Some things may seem hidden. However, God knows all things and sees all things. While you may seem alone in this dark place, you are never really all alone."

With that the room became black like blindness. Not a light or even a flicker. Ripley blinked her eyes trying to focus on something. Sight was gone. A deafening silence hushed the room. All she could hear was the beating of her heart throbbing within her ears like an old washing machine swishing blood. The room was empty. Compelled by fear, she ran blindly to get out of the room, but came up against a brick wall that knocked her down. "Let me out of here!" she screamed. "I can't see anything. Acacia, help me, help me; someone please let me out of this place of darkness." As she cried, she rolled around on the floor as if wrestling with herself. After exhausting herself, she just lay on the floor looking up into the darkness. *Why, oh God, have you kept me in this darkness? Give me eyes that I might see. Help me, God, to come out of this darkness.*

MY BELOVED, BE STILL AND KNOW THAT I AM GOD. REST IN THIS DARK PLACE RATHER THAN FIGHT IN IT. TRUST IN ME AND YOU WILL SEE AND UNDERSTAND THE WAYS OF YOUR GOD.

Ripley was reminded of the Psalm 139:1–12:

O Lord, you have searched me and you know me. You know when I sit and when I rise; you perceive my thoughts from afar. You discern my going out and my lying down; you are familiar with all my ways. Before a word is on my tongue you know it completely, O Lord. You hem me in—behind and before; you have laid your hand upon me. Such knowledge is too wonderful for me, too lofty for me to attain. Where can I go from your Spirit? Where can I flee from your presence? If I go up to the heavens, you are there; if I make my bed in the depths, you are there. If I rise on the wings of the dawn, if I settle on the far side of the sea, even there your hand will guide me, your right hand will hold me fast. If I say, "Surely the darkness will hide me and the light become night around me," even the darkness will not be dark to you; the night will shine like the day, for darkness is as light to you. (NIV)

Softly, a light appeared on the ceiling. It grew bigger and bigger until it filled the entire ceiling like a movie theatre screen. The soft light brought some relief from the black darkness, calming her. The calm quickly escalated and heat ran though her veins. Ripley's face flushed with the vision played on the ceiling. She saw herself in the dark room on the bed, recognizing it to be her bedroom from when she was a young girl. First she was sleeping in the bed. The clip changed. There was a man on top of her, holding her on the bed. His strong hands held her down. Ripley never saw his face in the darkness. It seemed masked. She remembered quite clearly the violation he inflicted upon her that night.

Up until this vision, she had blocked out that memory, or perhaps God had blocked that from her memory. All the feelings of helplessness, pain and fear she experienced that night came crashing back like a tidal wave. Reliving this memory, she watched the video play out, making her cry uncontrollably. Anger raged from the deepest part of her soul. She wanted to kill that man, whoever he was, this coward and rapist behind the mask. These feelings and thoughts she was having were the same feelings she had felt on that night as a fifteen-year-old girl. Questions invaded her mind. *Who would do that to me? Why did he inflict upon me such pain and invasion by taking something so personal from me? I don't understand.* The bedroom door opened. The light from the hallway seeped into the room. Hurriedly, the man ran out of the room when her mother entered, yelling at him. Ripley watched her mother come over to her and console her, telling her, "It is alright, honey. He is gone now. I'll take care of everything."

Her mother sat on the edge of the bed hugging Ripley and petting her long blond hair. "It will be okay, Ripley. He won't hurt you again. I'll see to that. You just close your eyes and try to get some sleep. Try to forget this ever happened. Hush, don't cry. It's okay." Ms. Wilks wiped away her daughter's tears until Ripley fell asleep.

The vision continued. This was a vision of an event that she never knew took place. Ripley watched her mother leave her bedside to go downstairs. Ms. Wilks walked into the kitchen and had a conversation with the man. The man had his back to her as he leaned over the kitchen counter. Her mother told the man to get out of the house and never come back or she would call the police and have him arrested. There was something so familiar to Ripley about this man. The rapist turned around, and to Ripley's surprise, she saw the face of her father. He pleaded with her mother to reconsider. He tried to make excuses in his drunken state by slurring his apologies, saying it wouldn't happen again. Ripley's mother was repulsed at what he had done. She told him, "Get out now. Get your suitcase and some clothes and leave. I want you gone before Ripley and Lauren wake up." Ripley watched the vision until it ended.

Ripley felt like there was a golf ball lodged in the pit of her stomach. Her heart sank, realizing that the face of the man behind the mask was her father. For years Ripley never knew the truth. All those years, she blamed her mother for the marriage break-up with her father. She never knew why her father left so quickly or why her family was suddenly divided. Her mother had only told her and her sister Lauren that their father had an affair with another woman. He never kept in touch with them after he left the house that day. For years, Ripley had felt so rejected by him leaving and never contacting them. Seeing this vision brought such a shock, a realization of the truth. Her stomach churned like sour milk, realizing the man she had hated and wanted to kill was her own father.

Ripley was always a tough shell, not really one for crying. Watching this vision, she started crying with such release. Lying on the floor, she travailed with deep pains like a woman giving birth. Warmth and a peace entered the room along with a glow and the presence of Holiness. A loving voice spoke to Ripley like a loving father would speak to a child.

FEAR NOT, RIPLEY: "FOR I AM WITH YOU; BE NOT DISMAYED, FOR I AM YOUR GOD: I WILL STRENGTHEN YOU, YES, I WILL HELP YOU, I WILL UPHOLD YOU WITH MY RIGHTEOUS RIGHT HAND. FOR I, THE LORD YOUR GOD, WILL HOLD YOUR RIGHT HAND, SAYING TO YOU, 'FEAR NOT, I WILL HELP YOU.'" (Isaiah 41:10–11, 13, NKJV).

Another vision appeared on the ceiling. It was her father, alone, feeling ashamed at the realization of what he had done in his drunkenness. He had his suitcase in hand, as he sat on a bench in the airport with a one-way ticket in hand. He put down his suitcase and his head fell into his hands as he hunched over, crying with remorse. Never again could he return. He didn't deserve a family or any happiness, so he thought. With his one-way ticket he boarded a plane to Utah. There he spent the next six years working every moment trying to bury his shame under stacks of paper and business deals. One act of indiscretion ripped his life apart. The sorrow he wore on his face etched the lines of disgrace. He didn't even have the answers to the why of what he had done. Ripley could hear his thoughts. *How could I have done that to my daughter? I loved her more than my life, but not more than my alcohol-induced lust. If there is a God, surely he would throw me into the pit of hell. That is what I deserve. My darling daughter, I will never be able to restore what I have taken from you. God have mercy on my soul. God, will you please be the Father to her that I cannot?*

Ripley was caught in an awkward place emotionally, feeling anger and pity toward her father, and she did not know how to respond.

5
Divided Heart

Ripley and Joseph drove down the long mountain road to get to the hospital. Snow banks three feet high edged the side of the road. The trees were white with the fresh snowfall from the previous night. Quiet conversation between them escalated when Roseway brought up the topic of the honeymoon.

"Maybe we should postpone the trip to Hawaii until Ripley is better."

"We have everything booked and I don't think we can get the money back if we cancel the flights now," Joseph reminded her. "The flights are scheduled for tomorrow and the cancellation deadline was two weeks ago. I think we should still go to Hawaii or we will lose all that money. Besides, it is our honeymoon and we have been waiting for this for two years. I really want to go with you. We can make love while looking out at the ocean. They say Hawaii is the place of love." Joseph was so passionate about the trip. He had dreamed about it for two years.

Roseway curled her lip in frustration, not knowing what to do. Her heart pulled both ways. "It sounds so romantic, and I want us to be together every day like we were last night. I just think that we should wait and see what Ripley's condition is like today. Then we will be able to make a right decision," she said, trying to be logical about the situation.

Joseph refused her idea. He didn't want to even think there was a possibility of not going on the honeymoon. "There is no decision to make. We are going on the honeymoon. We have waited all this time, planned every detail. We are going on the honeymoon."

Roseway was surprised by Joseph's strong tone and determination. She didn't respond because she felt the tears roll up in her throat, choking back any words of disagreement. His tone felt like a cutting blade to her heart. *Why is he being so selfish about this? Doesn't he care about Ripley? What about how I feel?* It reeled on her emotions like a fish pulling out a line and bending a fishing rod.

They pulled the car into the parking lot at the hospital and went in the main entrance. That same hospital atmosphere reminded her of her stay in the hospital a few years ago when she had a nervous breakdown, and when Ripley was in a coma the first time. It made her throat tighten like a hand was gripping it. A claustrophobic feeling made her light-headed. Now here she was again. That same fear of the unknown rested on her shoulders like a heavy yoke. They walked into the waiting room where Billy and Noreen greeted them with a hug.

Rose didn't waste any time. "Has the doctor been in yet? Is there any news on Ripley's condition?" Impatient for some resolve or a quick cure, she verbalized her frustration.

Billy replied. "Sorry Sis, not much news. The nurse said Doctor West would be in soon. They finished the scan and are setting Ripley up in a room as we speak."

"Mom, did you contact Ripley's mother?"

"Yes, Ms. Wilks and Lauren will be flying into Kelowna this afternoon."

Dr. West entered the room like he was walking the red carpet. "Hello, I'm Doctor West. We have taken a brain scan of Ripley to see what has caused her to collapse into a comatose state. It looks like a tumour has grown and it is pressing on some of the cranial nerves. We will have to remove the tumour before it causes any serious brain damage. The human body has a way of protecting itself, and that is why she is in a coma. Her brain has shut down to allow the body to fight off the tumour. The danger is that the longer she is in a coma, the more damage can be done. When her family arrives and we have the consent forms filled out, we will have the surgeon operate."

Roseway asked, "How dangerous is this operation? Could she die?"

"With any operation there is always a risk. The brain is very unpredictable. Our first concern is removing the tumour without causing more damage. Clotting can cause a lot of damage, serious paralysis and eventually death. For now we have her stabilized. The type of tumour is quite invasive and can be difficult to remove. Hopefully we will not get any surprises. That is all I can tell you at this time. If you are praying people, then you might want to pray."

Roseway plunked herself in the chair and stared at the green, tiled floor. Noreen quickly snapped Rose out of her daze. "Honey, Billy and I would like to go home to get some sleep. We have been here all night and we are exhausted. We need to get a ride home. Are you going to stay here a while?"

Joseph volunteered. "I'll drive you home. Rose can stay here with Ripley."

Noreen thanked Joseph. "That would be much appreciated. Rose, you could probably go in to see Ripley now that they have her in a room. We will also keep her in our prayers."

"Okay Mom, I'll talk to you later. I'll see if I can go in and stay with Ripley until her mother gets here."

Roseway sat by Ripley's bedside looking at Ripley. She looked like sleeping beauty lying there. Rose held her best friend's hand. She was tired from all the wedding preparations, and the emotional wedding day. The flip-flop of emotions and the way Joseph had spoken to her all made her feel depressed. Feeling the pulling of her heart strings was draining. Her thoughts scattered. *Did Joseph mean what he said about the honeymoon? I don't want to leave Ripley like this. Why can't he understand how I feel? It doesn't mean that I don't want to have a honeymoon. Under the circumstances, my heart would not be three-thousand miles away. It's just money. So what if we lose the money if we don't go? What if I lose my best friend? I have to be here for her. God, how am I going to tell Joseph that I don't want to go? How do I convince him without him getting angry with me? I was controlled by Big Joe my entire life. Now, for a moment, that red flag came up again when Joseph was adamant about going on the honeymoon. It was as if he gave me no choice. He made me feel that what I think and feel does not matter to him. God, I thought we would get married and live happily ever after. I dreamed of the perfect wedding day, not this. Why does everything always have to go wrong? Why is this happening to Ripley? When is it ever enough, God? It is like you enjoy seeing people unhappy and struggling. God, you could heal Ripley just like that if you wanted to.*

A still quiet voice said, ROSE, YOU ARE MY CHILD AND I LOVE YOU AND I LOVE RIPLEY. YOU DO NOT KNOW THE WAYS OF GOD. NOR DO YOU KNOW THE GOOD PURPOSE I HAVE FOR YOUR LIVES. ROSE, YOU DO KNOW THE TRUTH. ABIDE IN THE TRUTH AND THE TRUTH WILL ABIDE IN YOU. DO NOT FLEE FROM THE TRUTH. KEEP IT FIRMLY PLANTED IN YOUR HEART. LISTEN ONLY TO THE VOICE OF GOD. THE VOICE OF THE TRUTH WILL KEEP YOU FREE.

Within the quiet of the room, neither Ripley nor Rose spoke a word. In the corner of the room was a chair. Sitting on that chair was a little girl. She began to speak to Roseway. "Well Rosy, are you going to listen to that nonsense? Do you really believe all that God talk? You are right, Rose. Look at all the bad things that have happened in your life. I'm surprised you even believe there is a God at all. Was he ever really there when you needed him? Where was he when your mother was raped? Where was he when you were kidnapped by Big Joe? Where was God all the times Big Joe hit you? Where was God when Ripley was attacked by Big Joe? What about when Big Joe committed suicide? Need I go on and on and on?"

Rose looked dumbfounded. "Who are you? Who let you into the room?"

"Rosy, you let me into the room. Your own doubt let me into the room. You know that I have always been with you. I've been your companion for many years. You just couldn't see me. Today you can not only hear me, but you can see me. My name is Doubt. I'm your friend. You think God is your friend? Don't be silly."

Roseway snapped back, "You be quiet."

Joseph walked into the room at that moment. "Who are you telling to be quiet? Ripley couldn't be any quieter if she tried."

"That is not funny."

"I was just kidding. Who were you telling to be quiet?"

Changing the subject, Rose quickly answered. "No one." She tried to calm herself by talking in a softer tone. "I guess you dropped Mom and Billy off at home without any trouble."

"Yes, I did. No problem. Has there been any change in Ripley?"

"No, she just lies there like she is sleeping. I imagine Ms. Wilks and Ripley's sister Lauren will be here soon."

There was a pause in the conversation. Roseway bit her lip trying to get the courage to bring up the topic of the honeymoon again. She took a deep breath and blurted out, "I have to talk to you about the trip to Hawaii."

"What is there to talk about? The plane leaves tomorrow at 4 o'clock."

"Well, honey, I hope you can understand that I can't leave Ripley in this condition. I'm worried about her."

"I understand that you are worried. Worrying about her is not going to make her better. There is nothing you can do for her sitting by her bedside. It is our honeymoon, and it is important to me. That is why we can get on that plane and go."

"Joseph, I don't want to go. I've made up my mind, I'm not going. We can have a honeymoon here."

Sarcastically, Joseph taunted, "Oh, sure, why don't we pull up a bed right beside Ripley and make love here? That is so romantic. Wish I had of thought it."

"Joseph, you are being so selfish about this. I'm sorry you can't understand where I'm coming from."

"Well, I guess Ripley was right when she cautioned me about you being mature enough to be a wife."

"What are you talking about?"

"Right before Ripley collapsed, she was saying to me that she hoped us getting married wasn't too soon. She hoped that you were ready for the responsibility of being a wife. I'm beginning to think that she had a point."

"I'm ready to be a wife. This is not a normal circumstance. My best friend is lying in a coma and may not survive the operation. All you can think about is sex. To me that is being immature."

"It is not wrong for me to want to make love to my wife on our honeymoon in a nice romantic suite overlooking the ocean. We planned it, and waited for this special time together. You would choose to stay here with Ripley when you can't do a damn thing to help her. Sounds like you are choosing your friend over me."

Roseway raised her voice to match Joseph. "Joseph, that is not the truth and you know it. Please don't make it out to be something it is not."

The door opened and a nurse poked her head around the door. "Sorry to interrupt your loud conversation, but I must remind you that this is a hospital and the patient needs absolute quiet and peace. Please take your conversation elsewhere. Besides, there are two other people waiting to see Ripley. There are only two people per visit."

"Ms. Wilks and Lauren must be here. I'll go out to see them," Roseway said.

"I guess I have a few phone calls and cancellations to make," Joseph announced angrily. "I'll be down in the hospital lounge if you care to find me when you are finished speaking to Ripley's family."

"Okay Hun, I'll be down in a little while." Rose grabbed Joseph by the hand and tried to pull him close. "I love you."

Joseph was so angry with her that he didn't want to say another word. He pulled his hand out of hers to show his disapproval and walked out of the room.

Rose felt even more depleted. Her stomach sank with sadness and her eyes burned, holding back the tears. His pulling back hurt more than any words spoken.

Still sitting on the chair in the corner of the room, Doubt laughed. "Well that went well, don't you think? Now you have made Joseph angry with you. Way to ruin the honeymoon. Keep on like this and you are sure to destroy your marriage, too. Is that not what you do best, destroy relationships?"

With a disputing anger, Rose cursed, "Shut up, you little jerk!" Rose walked out of the room.

Ms. Wilks and Lauren were standing in the hall. She approached them with a sympathetic expression and asked if they had talked to the doctor. Ms. Wilks told Rose that they had signed the consent forms and that the doctor said they would be operating that night.

Ms. Wilks and Lauren entered into Ripley's room. They pulled up a chair by her bed. Ms. Wilks played with Ripley's blond hair. "She isn't going to be happy that they will be shaving all this beautiful blond silk off her head."

Lauren interjected, "I know, Mother. Ripley is so particular about her hair. What matters is that she pulls out of this. Mother, she has had such a difficult life already. She is so young. It just makes you wonder why so many things have happened to her."

Looking puzzled, Ms. Wilks said, "I don't have any answers. They say what doesn't kill you makes you stronger. She is one tough cookie. If anyone can beat this, Ripley can and will."

"I wish I was so sure. It sounds pretty bad."

"That is enough of the negative talk," Ms. Wilks demanded, denying any possibility of death or danger. They both stayed in the room with Ripley until the nurse came and took her away to prepare her for surgery.

6
Arms of Love

Still sitting, Ripley felt refreshed as she opened her eyes. Little Acacia was there beside her and they were in a new room. The room was decorated in soft blues and pinks. Acacia played a lullaby with her harp. Children sang along in the heavenly realm. Their childlike voices played like a perfectly tuned symphony in the distance. Ripley listened intensively, enjoying the serenity of the music to her ears. This room felt warm and comfortable. All the fear she was feeling earlier had disappeared. *What is this room?* Ripley thought to herself. *It is like being a baby safely wrapped in a blanket and being held in a mother's arms.*

Acacia told Ripley that God had another vision to show her. Acacia tried to prepare Ripley for the vision. "This vision might be upsetting. God is telling you not to forget the comforting feeling you just felt. He wants you to know that he has felt that same separation you have felt from your children. Ripley's eyes widened as she began to realize the vision he was going to show her. *I don't want to see this vision, if this is going to be the vision I think it is going to be. There is too much shame to watch. Just knowing that God is watching is more than I can bear. What did God mean when he said separation from my children?*

"Are you ready, Ripley, to walk a little further down this road of acceptance?" Acacia moved her wings and flew around Ripley.

Dust fell from her wings. Ripley closed her eyes. When she opened them, she recognized the grey, dingy clinic. She could smell the antiseptic. She remembered the nurse who wore a green mask over her face. Her brown eyes stared down at Ripley. The nurse was so close; Ripley could smell the coffee on her breath, seeping through the mask. Then the nurse told Ripley she would feel a little pinprick. When she awoke it would be all over. Feelings of fear permeated her body. A song kept playing within her mind, *Sweet baby of mine.* Ripley didn't want it to be over. She didn't want any of this.

It was her mother's decision that Ripley had an abortion. When Ripley was raped by her father, she conceived a child. Ms. Wilks could not allow a scandal. There was enough talk among the high society friends about Mr. Wilks leaving town. The stories they told gossiping grew like a bushfire out of control. If they ever heard of Ripley being pregnant at fifteen, she could only imagine what gossip would be spread. Ripley recalled all the reasons her mother had told her to convince her that abortion was the only option. Singing to herself, she stared at the green wall, feeling cold and helpless as she fought the medication to try and stay awake.

Now she watched the procedure like a fly on the wall. She remembered the needle and falling into a shallow sleep. The faint noises she heard during the procedure haunted her many nights. Every time someone turned on a vacuum cleaner, it made her cringe. The suction noise when she had her teeth cleaned at the dentist disturbed her greatly. Watching young mothers with their babies made her sad. She had never understood why until now, watching the vision and hearing these familiar noises she had heard as they removed the baby from her womb. To watch this vision almost made her sick.

Why, God, do you want me to watch this vision? Is it to make me feel even more remorseful than I already feel?

As if Acacia knew what she was thinking, she told Ripley, "God is showing you this vision so that you can know his forgiveness. He loves you and is willing to forgive all your sins. In seeing this vision, you will be able to help other women who have not been able to face their pain. In this same way you can help other women realize that there is an alternative to abortion. Ripley, God also wants to show you what you did not see. For only God knows the entire picture. Close your eyes again, Ripley, as I play the harp again. Listen closely to the children's voices singing so beautifully."

The music played again. Ripley was given a vision of a choir of children. There were thousands upon thousands of children singing in this choir. Each one had a perfect little face. Boys and girls singing like sparrows. Her eyes welled up with tears listening to the sound and looking at their angelic faces, bright, smiling with such joy. Standing in the front row of the choir was a little boy and a little girl. For some reason she felt drawn to them. There was an undeniable connection she felt toward them—a bond like you would find between a mother and her child. Her face flushed as she realized that those two children were her unborn babies and they were singing in the biggest heavenly choir there could be. Tears rolled down Ripley's face. *These are my children? There were two babies, not one? Oh God.*

Acacia told Ripley that God named them Josiah and Jasmine. God also gave names to all the other children.

"Oh my, the choir of children represents all the babies who died at a young age," Ripley concluded.

"That is right, Ripley. As you have witnessed, your children are with God. They are loved beyond words. Happiness is their reward. The psalm reminds us how great God is when he says: *I praise you because I am fearfully and wonderfully made; your works are wonderful, I know that full well. My frame was not hidden from you when I was made in the secret place. When I was woven together in the depths of the earth, your eyes saw my unformed body. All the days ordained for me were written in your book before one of them came to be* (Psalm 139:14–16, NIV).

"The psalmist also says: *Sons are a heritage from the Lord, children a reward from him*" (Psalm 127:3, NIV).

"How can I be of help to other women? Who would listen to me?" Ripley asked.

The vision ended and the voice of God spoke softly, "MY GRACE IS SUFFICIENT FOR YOU, FOR MY STRENGTH IS MADE PERFECT IN WEAKNESS. WHEN YOU CAN ACCEPT MY TOTAL FORGIVENESS, YOU WILL EASILY FORGIVE YOUR FATHER, MOTHER AND YOURSELF FOR THE DECISIONS MADE. YOU WILL BE MORE THAN ABLE TO HELP OTHERS."

Ripley found herself back in the blue and pink room. She sat at a table and held a little baby blanket up close to her face. Feeling the softness on her face she smiled at the thought of a baby. There was a little teddy bear on the table, and she picked it up and pretended to make it dance, talking to the little bear like she was entertaining her baby. Ripley looked up at Acacia and said, "That is incredible that God showed me my babies. There are so many women who never get that privilege. Father God gave them names. I never had the chance to do that. I like the names God chose for them. If only I could hold them in my arms and tell them I love them and that I'm sorry.

"I would sing them a song like this one: *Now as I reflect back to the past. Years ago, yet it seems like only yesterday when I was caught in a world of upside downs, empty faces all around. It seemed like there was no where I could turn. If I could erase that day; what can I say? My words are few. I never had the chance to say I love you. I know that there is a heaven. I know that you are with the Lord. I know that God the Father loves you and that you are wrapped in the arms of God's love. Now I must look ahead and gather all the things I've learned along the way. In this world life goes on; the struggles make us strong. I'll take what I've learned and help someone else along. So I speak to you today. What can I say, my words are few. I just want to tell you that I love you."*

Acacia spoke softly, "Oh Ripley, they know you love them. They heard and felt your love when they looked at you and you looked at them. Your heart told them how much you love them and that you are sorry. It is beneficial to know and understand that they are in heaven now. Josiah and Jasmine know a love divine. They are wrapped in God's loving arms."

Ripley looked so happy to realize this to be true. "Yes, they are. Praise be to God.

7
Behind Closed Doors

Acacia took Ripley into another room. Musical notes and artistic paintings covered the walls. This room had an exciting feeling about it. Ripley herself was very artistic and creative. She could play the piano and was a talented singer. In this room, there was a piano made of cherry wood. It had an acrylic shine that sparkled from the light. The legs on the piano were bronze and shaped like the feet of a lion. The keys were made of smooth marble, soft to the touch. Ripley sat down on the piano bench and pulled herself close. She rubbed her fingers together and sang a worship song that she had composed. The words flowed from her lips like a sweet breath.

The sound from the piano was amazingly beautiful, yet somewhat different from any piano she had ever played. Even her voice was perfect, with no trace of notes being out of key. She actually impressed herself with the sound. *I've never played the piano so good. Never has my voice sounded so perfect. I like this place.* Her heart was still overwhelmed from the visions she had seen and the words God had spoken to her that she just wanted to sing praises and worship to him. The love she felt from him was like nothing she had ever felt before. It compelled her to want to love him back with her song.

"Holy, Holy! Thou art Holy! Holy, Holy! Lamb of God. Jesus, Jesus my Redeemer. Jesus, Jesus my precious Lord. I love you with all of my heart. I love you with all of my mind. I love you with all of my strength. Lord, you are the air I breathe. Your fountain of life washes over me again and again. There is no greater love than yours. You laid your life down for mine. You gave to me a gift so sweet; a gift of Greater Love. I give back to you my love, in the presence of your Holiness. With praise on my lips, my tears in your hands, on bended knees I bow before thee."

Ripley worshiped and sang love songs to God for a long time. Time did not seem to matter. There were no clocks in this place, and she was quite content to stay in this room of love forever. It felt so right, and the essence of God's Holiness filled the room.

Acacia flew into the room as the music began to fade, and gave a message to Ripley. "Dear Ripley, Father God is well pleased with you and He loves your praises and worship. God loves how you love Him. It pleases Him that you are beginning to realize that His love and grace is beyond compare.

"It has been your struggle to find love in the wrong places, in the wrong people and in the wrong ways. As you are beginning to realize, you have not been alone in your struggles. Sometimes your behaviour has grieved God, but His grace is sufficient to forgive. Our Father knows the struggle you are going through at this time. There is one more vision God wants to show you to enable you to overcome this sinful desire that has plagued you for quite some time. Ripley, this is the last vision. It will lead you to the end of your road of acceptance. You have made so much progress so far on your journey. I know it has not been easy. You have overcome the childhood misconceptions which only fed your insecurities. Through this experience, you have learned that if we look beyond what we see, often our entire perspective will change.

"The violation and incest you endured attacked your womanhood and caused you to put up walls of protection. These walls really didn't protect you at all. They only confused you. That confusion hindered you from becoming the woman God has intended you to become.

"The shame, sorrow and the separation you felt from having an abortion changed your life in such a demeaning way. The lack of worth you felt about yourself drove you to run away from everyone to live a life in the dumpster of denial. That is where you sought to fill the void in your life in ungodly ways. That lifestyle is all you felt worthy of having. God has shown you that in his eyes you are of great worth to Him. That is why He stayed in the dumpster with you. He also allowed you to make your own choices. Even still, God worked his wonders in many ways to bring you from that place of bondage, and by bringing Roseway into your life. When you are ready, Ripley, you may choose to open this final door and walk the rest of the journey on the road to acceptance."

Ripley stood up from the piano bench and put her hand on the door knob, and paused. *Do I want to see another vision? Or should I go back now? I can't even imagine what the rest of this journey will be like. God wouldn't take me to a place for no good reason. There is always a purpose.*

She took no more time to ponder what she should do. Deep down inside her spirit, Ripley knew she had to open the door.

Walking through the open door, she found herself back in Prince George at the age of seventeen. She had just been kicked out of the house by her mother. Ever since the abortion, Ripley and her mother could never get along. Ripley had felt so much anger toward her mother for coercing her to have the abortion. She got in with the wrong crowd at high school and smoking drugs became the norm. It helped ease the pain, made her feel good. At the same time, it made her very difficult to get along with. Ms. Wilks had enough of the disrespect, the broken curfews. Ripley also had enough of her mother and the high society lifestyle. Feeling bitter and angry at all of society, she left home to live on the streets.

Ripley remembered the thoughts she had that day as a seventeen-year-old as she leaned against the brick wall. *What will Mother's high society friends have to say now? Mother will be so embarrassed. Wonder how she will explain to them why I'm living on the street. Her daughter is a street bum. All I have ever been to her is an embarrassment, unlike Lauren, who was always the perfect daughter. Her and Mother were always close. Why did Dad have to move away? Wish he had of taken me with him. He and I were always close. I guess he couldn't stand Mother either. That is why he ran away with some other woman.*

Leaning against the wall, she watched all the people walking here and there. *As if they all have some place to go. Look at that idiot dressed in his three-piece suit. He should be going to a funeral. Oh, and that lady with her little kids. I bet she beats them when she gets them home. Oh, look at this one coming. Maybe I'll just stick my foot out and trip her. Hey, I can do whatever I want now. There is no one to boss me around anymore.*

Before Ripley could allow the thoughts to process, out went her foot and down went this young woman, tumbling onto the cement sidewalk. She went down hard, hitting her knee on the ground, scraping the skin from her kneecap. Blood rolled down her leg. Ripley felt a little surprise along with a little remorse for what she had done as the woman sat on the ground holding her leg in pain.

"Oh, I'm sorry. Are you okay? I didn't..."

Holding back her tears and clenching her teeth in pain, the woman forced a reply. "Don't worry about it. I guess I should have been watching where I was going. Could you give me a hand up?"

"Sure," Ripley responded, feeling more than guilt for having tripped her.

"I'm afraid my leg is pretty banged up. I can't seem to walk. Could you be so kind as to help me get to my place? It is just around the corner. I live in a little brownstone building on 5th Avenue."

Ripley put the woman's arm around her neck and helped her hobble down the street.

The wounded woman was in her early twenties, frail looking, yet pretty with her jet black hair and long-lashed blue eyes. They reached the brownstone and Ripley helped her up the stairs and into her house. The woman thanked Ripley for her kindness and invited her to stay for a cup of tea.

"By the way, my name is Abigail. You can call me Abby for short."

Bitterly, with some sarcasm, Ripley replied, "Is that like Dear Abby? Maybe you could give me some advice, Dear Abby."

"Sure, I could give you some advice, but you might not like my advice."

"I was just kidding. Last thing I want is some advice from a stranger."

Trying to break through Ripley's bitter tone and saucy attitude, Abby asked, "What is your name?"

"My name is Ripley."

"There, Ripley, now we know each other's name, so I guess we are not strangers anymore. Where do you live?"

"Right now, I don't live anywhere. I just got told to leave home by my mother."

"No kidding."

"I wouldn't kid about that."

"Why did your mother kick you out of the house?"

"We got in a little fight. She caught me and a couple friends smoking marijuana in the house. She said that was the last straw. If I couldn't abide by her rules, then out I would have to go. I told her that is fine with me. I don't need her rules, her money or her stupid friends."

"Well, that may have been a little rash of a decision for you to make."

"Maybe, but here I am on the street, no money, no friends, nothing."

Abby's mind kept thinking, *Get this girl out of here.* However, her compassionate heart told her to help. Before she could stop from speaking, an invitation flowed from her lips. "I'll be your friend. You can stay here for a little while until you figure out some other arrangement. Like your mother, I won't put up with any drugs in this place. What you do outside is your business. I run a little music business out of this house. I have students coming and going and I can't have any nonsense going on. If you can respect my place and me, then it won't be a problem. What do you think?"

"That is very kind of you to offer. I can't pay you anything."

"I know that."

"Why are you being so nice?" Ripley couldn't believe her kindness. *She must be on crack*, she thought to herself.

"I'm a pretty good judge of character. I think you are someone who could use a little break. I don't want to see you on the street. However, if you would rather live on the cold street, hungry and penniless, well, that is your decision."

"Would you be so kind to me even if you knew I tripped you on purpose?"

"Yes, I know you did. That is another reason I want to help you. I can see you have a lot of hurt and anger bottled up inside of you."

"You seem to have good insight, Abby. So, you are a music teacher and a fortune-teller." Ripley laughed.

"Yes, I am a music teacher. It doesn't take a fortune-teller to know you have some problems. It is written all over your countenance. If you want to help yourself, you may want to get rid of the attitude."

Ripley sat quietly for a moment after receiving her rebuke. Then she softened her tone of voice. "You know what? I play a little piano myself."

Abby looked intrigued. "Is that right? Hmm ... I am working on a recording at the studio. I'm hoping I get a contract with a label. Maybe we could write some songs together. Would you like to sit down at the piano? I'll play my guitar. Can you play this song?" Abby picked up her guitar and started playing a song from the book.

Ripley watched the vision. The memory of her and Abby singing put a smile on her face that stretched from ear to ear. They jammed every night and wrote quite a few songs together that year. Ripley even helped some of Abby's students with their vocals. Abby and Ripley became the closest of friends. They dressed in funny clothes and went to parties with people in the music business.

Then Abby met Ted Nash. He was influential in the music industry, and quite the ladies man. Abby was swept away by Ted's suave mystique. There was something about Ted that Ripley didn't like; something so very pretentious. She could see that Abby had the blinders on. Whatever Ted told Abby was the gospel truth as far as Abby was concerned. He promised her the moon all wrapped up in a nice record deal.

Ripley told Abby how she felt about Ted. Abby just snuffed it off as jealousy. She was partially right, Ripley was jealous. Abby truly believed that Ted loved her and that her songs would make a hit record.

The longer the relationship went on, the more things didn't add up. Ripley watched Ted like a hawk. She had grown to really love Abby, and she was not going to let anyone hurt her. Within that year, Ted Nash had broken off with Abby and in the process stolen her songs, giving them to another prominent singer. Abby was devastated. Her spirit was crushed. Ripley tried to help her by covering for her with some of the music students. Abby was so depressed she didn't want to get out of bed.

One morning, Ripley made Abby a nice breakfast and took it in to her. Abby met Ripley's eyes with such a look—a connection of the soul. "Thank you for making breakfast for me. You have been working so hard taking care of the house. I really appreciate you covering for me with the students. You treat me so great." Abby's eyes watered with gratitude.

"You are welcome, Abby. I know you have been going through a hard time. Ted really broke your heart. He was such an idiot. You deserve better than him, someone who really loves you."

Abby did want to be loved. She felt so empty and sad. "I don't think I'll ever find that person." She started to cry.

Ripley sat on the bed beside her to console her with a hug. "I love you." Then she wiped the tears from Abby's face.

A spark of truth in Ripley's statement entered Abby's mind. "I believe you do love me, Ripley." Without hesitation, Abby put her hand on Ripley's and then she touched Ripley's face.

Their touches gave them a feeling they didn't expect.

"I love you too, Ripley."

Ripley kissed Abby on the cheek. Abby enjoyed the love she felt coming from Ripley and she reciprocated. That morning, their relationship was changed by the experience. They both felt emotions they had never felt before. Throughout the day they busied themselves with students and preoccupied themselves doing things apart from each other.

The next morning, Abby came into Ripley's room. Ripley smiled at Abby, feeling an even stronger bond toward her. "Good morning."

Abby's face looked pale and serious as she held a suitcase in her hand. "Ripley, it is time that you leave."

"Leave? What do mean, leave? Why? Is it because of what happened yesterday?"

"Yes, it is. That is all I have been able to think about since yesterday morning. I can't allow anything more to grow out of that kiss. I know that if I allow you to stay here, it will. I can't deny that I was very moved. However, I believe it is so wrong. We should not have done that. I'm so sorry. I was just feeling so vulnerable. I don't understand what came over me."

"It is okay. I do love you, but we don't have to let that happen again."

"No, it is not okay, because I think I have fallen in love with you. I thought about it all night long. I never slept a wink last night. I'm a Christian and I know what God says about homosexuality. While it may be accepted by most people these days, I know that God does not change his opinion. His word is truth. I wanted to find some way to condone what we did, because I don't want to lose you or your friendship. I kept coming up with the same answer, that it is so wrong... It is like taking something that seems good, but you know it is poison. I don't know how my family and friends would react. My parents are strong Christians. I don't believe that they would be able to accept you and me as a couple. I don't believe God would be pleased. An apple is an apple, no matter how much we want to call it an orange. Sin is sin no matter how much we desire it.

"I'm sorry, Ripley, but I can't see you again. Our friendship has changed because of what we did. It doesn't mean I don't still love you, because I do. The right thing to do at this time is to part company."

Ripley was dumbfounded. She couldn't believe what Abby was saying. "What are you talking about? We have a wonderful friendship. You are the best friend I ever had. Please don't allow what happened to ruin our friendship."

Abby was adamant. "Ripley, I have to go out this morning. Here is some money to help you find a place. Please pack yourself whatever clothing you want. You can have this suitcase, and please be gone when I get back. If you really love me, then you will go."

Abby softly laid the suitcase on the bed. She leaned over and touched Ripley's hand and kissed her on the cheek, then walked out of the room, closing the door behind her.

Ripley's heart was broken. She couldn't believe how their friendship had fallen apart. The confusion she felt about everything that had happened between them left her with many questions. The experience of the moment didn't repulse her; however, it did leave her feeling somewhat strange. All she really wanted was to love her friend and be loved in return. Never in her imagination did she think she would find herself involved in that way. It happened so fast. Both of their needs and the vulnerability they felt from life's hurts lead them to the place of unfamiliarity and experimentation. Now the very thing she had desired was gone from her life. Dragging herself out of bed, she got dressed and packed the suitcase with a few pieces of clothing that Abby had given to her. As she packed, her thoughts compiled. *Abby's friendship was the first time I ever really felt loved and cared for by someone. It has turned out so wrong. I can't believe she wants me to leave. How can she end our friendship just like that? Where will I go now? I'm not going home to Mother.*

Ripley continued to watch the vision with tear-filled eyes. She never knew what happened to Abby after that day. Now, in the vision she watched Abby leave the brownstone. The tears rolling down Abby's face, distraught, confused and so despaired. In the moment, Abby felt reckless and didn't care about anything. The morning rush-hour traffic filled the downtown streets. Abby wasn't concentrating on anything but the conversation she just had with Ripley.

Within the blink of an eye, she was struck by a car and went airborne, finding herself lying on the cold cement road.

In the vision, God showed Ripley a convalescence home. There was Abby in rehabilitation, painfully trying to walk again. When the car hit Abby, it had broken the femurs in both her legs. Ripley cried as she watched the vision, saddened by her friend's condition. Regret and guilt tried to rest on Ripley's shoulders as she watched her crippled friend struggling to walk.

The vision faded out like a movie coming to an end. Ripley prayed, *O God, you have searched me, and you know my heart—tested me and know my anxious thoughts. O God, you have witnessed my offensive ways and you love me and forgive me. Lord, I know your greater love. Who else would die for my sins? Who else would forgive me for the things I have done? None but you, Lord; none but you. I think what you are showing me through watching these life events is the condition of the human heart. Your bible tells us that all have sinned and fall short of the glory of God. Each of us must accept ourselves the way you, God, accept us. It is the sinful nature and our sinful lusts and desires that we must forsake. When we do that, we can easily accept your love and forgiveness. I need to accept myself just the way I am. Your love, oh God, endures forever. While the love of others can fade or depart us, your love, oh God, endures all things.*

The next thing Ripley knew, she was sitting in the most beautiful garden surrounded by plants with large, leaf-like stems.

Different kinds of flowers with many shapes, colours and sizes surrounded her. A gazelle drank from a nearby pond. A lion lay peacefully by the edge of the pond. Ripley looked in awe at the beauty all around her.

Acacia flew down and sat beside her and spoke lovingly. "Well Ripley, as you can see, the road to acceptance has lead you to the most beautiful of gardens—to the Garden of Eden, which means paradise, bliss or delight. God has set before you a choice. You can travel the road of life for eternity or you can go back to your life as you know it on earth. If you choose to go back, life will be unpredictable. However, you have learned acceptance. That acceptance can be your friend on your earthly journey. Your journey will need acceptance, for it will be another challenging road. You can use what God has shown you through the visions to help yourself and to also help others who have faced similar challenges.

"We will leave you in the garden until you decide which road you want to choose."

8
THE CHOICE

The surgeon and nurses prepared for surgery to attempt the removal of Ripley's tumour. In the waiting room was Ms. Wilks, Lauren, Roseway, Joseph, Noreen and Ripley's boyfriend JD. Four hours went by, and Ripley was still in surgery. The doctors were having difficulty removing the tumour, as it had grown amongst some delicate nerves. It was a dangerous procedure. The slightest mistake could cause severe damage.

Time seemed to stand still as they all waited. The room was so quiet. Everyone jumped when Ms. Wilks broke the silence. "Ripley was never afraid of a good fight. She will be just fine. She will fight her way back from this, too. I remember when she was in grade six. This eighth grade student Helga Bonsacker picked a fight with her because she ran through their skipping rope. I'm sure this big bully thought she would have some fun intimidating Ripley. Ripley surprised her and overpowered the girl until the teacher came along. Helga was so mad that she ended up beating up the teacher."

Lauren remembered a story, too. "Mother, do you remember our camping trip with Dad up at Blackcomb? We hadn't been there more than a half an hour when Ripley fell off her bike and scraped her leg from one end to the other. The blood was running down her leg. She rode her bike all the way back to camp, in such pain. Then

Dad had to pick all the stones out of her leg. She was back riding that bicycle not long after he bandaged her up. Nothing got in her way of having some fun. Ripley was always strong-willed. I know that strong will is what will bring her back to us."

* * *

"We have a code blue!" The nurse yelled as the heart monitor flat lined. "Get the defibrillator paddles—one, two, three, clear." Jolts of electricity zapped Ripley's body.

* * *

Acacia arrived back at the garden. "It is time, Ripley, to make a choice. What path do you want to take now? You have journeyed the road of acceptance. Now you can go back to your family and friends and face some of the biggest challenges you have yet to endure. Or do you wish to come with me now and journey through to eternity now and for all time? Which road do you want to choose? You have gained a new insight into the meaning of life. God has shown you his divine perspective. With God's strength combined with your faith, there is nothing you cannot overcome.

Ripley paused for only a moment. Like a pulling of a magnet, Ripley felt she wanted to go back to her life, whatever it would be.

9
The Diagnosis

Doctor Brown spoke to the surgical team. "We've got her back. There is still one small tumour left to remove. It is too close to the temporal lobe. We might do more harm than good if we try to remove it. We will monitor her condition. Hopefully there will be minimal paralysis. Let's get this closed and get her to the Intensive Care Unit, then I will go and consult the family about her condition."

Doctor Brown removed his mask and gloves and went to clean up. Ms. Wilks and the others waited until the doctor came out to speak with them. "Hello, I'm Doctor Brown. Ripley is out of surgery now. It looks like it went well. She should be awakening within the next few hours. She was heavily sedated and the surgery was extensive. It took longer than anticipated. We did lose her once during the operation. Perhaps your prayers brought her back. Anyway, we won't know for a few days just how much nerve damage has been done. Nurses are monitoring her closely."

The following day, Ripley awoke from the coma and was recovering from surgery. Roseway was able to spend some time with Ripley. Ripley was paralyzed from the waist down, and had partial paralysis in her arms. Doctors were hopeful that she would regain some of the feeling over time, but did not know if or how long this would take. By training the other parts of her brain, and with the healing of some of the nerves, there was a fifty percent chance of her regaining the feeling in her arms.

For the first few days, it was difficult for Ripley to speak as they removed a tube from her throat. Her thoughts were scattered and she didn't make sense. Rose didn't care, she was just so happy to see her friend alive.

Roseway held Ripley's hand, but there was no response as her hand lay limp within hers. "Ripley, can you feel any sensation in your hand?"

Ripley whispered, "Not really. It is a strange feeling. I want to wiggle my toes, but I can't. My nose is itchy, but I can't scratch it. I want to hug you back, but I can't."

Roseway calmed her by caressing her cheeks and wiping away the tear that rolled down her face. She scratched Ripley's nose.

Ripley wanted to tell Roseway about her experience. It was still fresh in her memory. "Rose, when I was in a coma, my spirit left my body and I was in heaven. God showed me all these visions of my life. They were so difficult to watch. God showed me such love and forgiveness that is hard to describe. It was amazing. I could have stayed there, but I chose to come back, not knowing that I would have to live with this disability. I never imagined my life would be like this. I feel trapped in this body. God is trying to teach me a lesson in acceptance, which is more difficult than any lesson yet. This is something beyond my control. It has nothing to do with my sin or what I have done. It just is and it is part of God's plan."

"That is amazing, Ripley. You were truly in heaven? What is heaven like? Did you see God? What visions did you have?"

Ripley's face brightened at the thought. She began to describe Acacia. She tried to explain the feelings she had when she first realized she was in heaven. As she started to describe some of the rooms she experienced, their conversation was interrupted.

JD walked into the room with a bouquet of flowers for Ripley. Her eyes lit up with surprise. Roseway left the room so they could be alone.

JD looked with a little surprise when he immediately noticed Ripley's bald head. He tried to hide his expression. Ripley could clearly read it. Feeling self-conscious, she tried to cover her head with her hands. She started to cry.

JD reached over her and kissed her. "It's okay, Ripley. I love you. We will get through this together. You look beautiful even without hair. I was just surprised."

"I may never walk again. It's not okay. I can't even hug you."

"Maybe not, but you can kiss me." He kissed her again and she kissed him back.

"Oh, John..." she said softly. "Can you honestly see yourself spending your life with a cripple?"

"Honey, how can you ask that question of me? Do you really think me to be so shallow? I will help you get better. I'll go to therapy with you. Let's take one day at a time. Rome was not built in a day."

"How long before you have to go back to teach?"

I've had Professor Jenkins substituting for me for the last few days. I'll have to go back to Prince George tomorrow. We are working on getting you transferred to Prince George for rehabilitation. When you get there, I'll be able to help you."

She sighed with a deep breath. "I'm so glad you came. Will you just hold me until you have to leave? You smell so great. I love you."

"I love you, too, sweetheart."

JD stayed with her for a few hours and lay on the bed beside her until he had to leave for his flight. He kissed her goodbye and encouraged her that he would see her soon. He walked out of the room, took out a handkerchief and wiped his eyes, feeling the damage like it were his own.

Ripley was somewhat different in her personality. Though she was given a meagre diagnosis and knew the challenges ahead of her were going to be difficult, she had a divine understanding of God's bigger plans and a sense of acceptance that no one else could understand. She didn't like what she had become in the physical, but in the spiritual she knew there was a purpose in everything that happens. For the next few months, she would be in an extensive care rehabilitation program in Prince George to help her learn to cope with her disability, while also taking chemotherapy and steroids to shrink the remaining tumour.

10
The Voice of Doubt

Roseway left Ripley in the room with J.D. She had remained strong in front of her friend, but when she left the room she leaned against the hospital wall and fell down to the floor and gushed like a broken dam. *Oh God, why, why have you allowed this to happen to Ripley? She doesn't deserve this hand that was dealt to her. God, you have to heal her.*

"Oh Rosy," Doubt sneered. "Maybe you will listen to me now. God's not going to heal Ripley. Why would he do that? It is impossible. There was too much damage done to her brain. She will be in a wheelchair for the rest of her life. No more walks on the beach for the two of you. All that fun the two of you used to have is gone. She will be more of a burden to you than a friend. Besides, shouldn't you get home to Joseph and try and make some peace with him? He is so furious with you for not going on the honeymoon. He is probably wondering why he ever married you in the first place. When he goes on one of those truck trips, he might even pick up another stray girl. I bet she would please him."

Roseway held her hands over her ears, with tears streaming down her face. Then she looked at Doubt sitting on the floor across from her. "You are a liar. I won't listen to your lies."

Roseway got up and ran down the hall and out of the hospital doors. She called Joseph to pick her up and take her home.

Joseph drove up to the entrance doors where Roseway was waiting, sitting on the curb with her head resting in her hands. He honked the horn to get her attention. She ran over to the car and quickly got in and closed the door. The drive seemed longer than usual without any conversation. They both went into the house without saying a word.

For weeks the conversation between Joseph and Rose was stalled. It was weighing on Rose. She desperately wanted to break down that wall between them. Roseway prepared a chicken and rice casserole, lit a couple of candles and strategically placed them on the table. She put on some soft instrumental music, hoping it might break the mood Joseph was wallowing in. The silence between them was eating away at her like a termite gnawing on wood. It had been weeks and Joseph was still giving her the cold shoulder. She wanted to discuss so many things with him. Hunger burned in the pit of her stomach as she longed to feel his strong arms around her, holding her tight. She fantasized about having his gentle kisses brushing the softness of her neck.

They sat down at the table. Usually, Joseph would say a prayer before they ate. This night he didn't even feel like saying that. He just dug his fork into the food and ate. Roseway couldn't take another minute of silence, and tried to break the tension. "Honey, would you like some water with your dinner?"

"No."

Roseway just started talking regardless of his abrupt reply. "Well, aren't you curious to know how Ripley is doing?"

He forced a reply. "I know how she is doing. I talked to Lauren."

"Oh, I didn't know that. I feel so bad. Ripley may never walk again. There has been little improvement since the operation." Roseway wanted so much to tell Joseph how sad she felt. That it was tearing her apart. She was trying to tell him how she felt, hoping for a little sympathy. All he wanted to do was attack her character and her loyalty to Ripley.

"Do you feel bad for her, or for yourself?"

His implication was like a hit in the face and Roseway tried to defend herself. "What do you mean? Of course I feel bad for her. How can you ask that question?"

"I don't know. I was just wondering. By the way, did you know that they will be taking Ripley to rehabilitation in Prince George in a couple of days?" He wanted to see Roseway feel that hurt he was harbouring. Joseph's attempt worked because it made her feel sad and surprised.

"No, I didn't think it would be that soon."

Changing the subject, Joseph inflicted another surprise poke. "I'll be leaving first thing tomorrow morning. I have a shipment to take to Oregon."

"But I thought..."

"You thought what? You don't expect me to sit around the house and do nothing while you spend all your time at the hospital every day. After all, we didn't go on our honeymoon. Someone has to pay for the cancellation fees."

"Joseph, are you ever going to forgive me? I'm sorry you feel so disappointed. I am disappointed, too. I just thought ... well you know how I felt. This is silly. You hardly talk to me. We haven't made love since our wedding night. Your constant verbal jabs make me feel like you are punishing me."

Joseph continued to eat his dinner, thinking about what she said. He was so disappointed that he wanted to stay mad at her.

Looking at her sparkling eyes and the little pout on her lip endeared her to him. He hadn't thought of his behaviour toward her as being punishing. He began to let down his wall of defence. The flickering glow from the candles made her hair shimmer. As she reached for her water glass, his hand fell upon hers. He grabbed her hand and pulled her off of her chair and into his lap. He kissed her deeply. They both responded with passion and desire. They stood up from the chair as they removed each other's clothing. He nudged her against the cupboard, still kissing.

The house had many windows. Suddenly, Roseway saw a shadow run passed the window. An old-time fear arose within her as she interrupted what they were doing. "Joseph, did you see that? There is someone outside, watching us through the window."

Joseph was aroused and kept kissing on her breast, ignoring her concern. "Don't be silly, we are way out here. There is nobody around."

"Please, Joseph, stop. Will you please have a look outside for me and make sure?"

Joseph took a big sigh of frustration and broke their contact. He went to the door, putting his shirt back on, and walked out into the darkness of night. Every star glimmered like diamonds in front of the black sky. He flicked on the outside light, then looked around. Cold air made him shiver. Entering the house, he snarled, "You are paranoid. There is no one out there. What is it with you lately? I catch you talking to yourself, and now you are seeing things."

"I'm telling you, I saw someone go passed the window. I would feel more comfortable if we made love in the bedroom."

"I'm no longer in the mood," he snapped. "Besides, I have to go map out my route for tomorrow morning."

Joseph walked out of the kitchen and into the other room. Rose sat on the chair at the kitchen table staring at her empty glass.

That is how she felt, just like an empty glass. Her stomach burned with desire for him. She spun the glass around in her hand, squeezing it tight. The glass shattered in her hand. Blood ran through her fingers. Quickly, she ran over to the sink and put her hand under cold water to wash away any glass and blood.

While she rinsed her hand, her memory slipped back to her childhood. She remembered being at the cabin with Big Joe. *He was showing her how to throw knives and axes. They practiced every day. One day, Big Joe told Rose to stand against the tree and not to move or flinch while he practiced throwing the knife. He wanted to put his skills to the test and Rose had no choice but to help him. He told her to put her arms out to the side and hold them still. Rose closed her eyes, afraid he would hit her. The knife flew through the air and landed in the tree right beside Rose's body. He took another knife and threw it to the other side of her waist. It landed solidly in the tree. Taking the third knife, he threw it. Rose felt the flesh slice under her arm. The knife had caught the edge of Rose's arm. It started to bleed profusely. Big Joe rushed to her. Ripping the shirt off of his back, he wrapped it around her arm, saying, "Rose, you moved your arm. Let this be a lesson in trust."*

Roseway snapped herself back as she watched the blood flow down the sink into the drain.

Joseph, now calm, came back into the kitchen to finish what they had started earlier. By this time, Roseway was tired from her emotional day and the game of push and shove she felt he was playing. Joseph told her to come to bed. She cleansed and dressed for bed and slid herself under the blankets, not really feeling very amorous. Joseph was determined to exercise his manly right without giving much pleasure to Roseway. He was behaving so differently than on their wedding night, and Roseway was reacting to the coldness emanating from him. Though he received a release, it was less than fulfilling to Roseway as she felt more like he had taken something from her that was not given freely, that she had been pressured to comply. It left her feeling disappointed and somewhat used. It was certainly nothing like the romantic bliss they shared on their wedding night. It boggled her mind, thinking about it as she lay there looking at the darkness, crying silently. When he finished, he rolled over and dispassionately turned his back to her. For a brief moment, her mind wondered why they had married. Their relationship seemed strained since the wedding day. It had changed in a negative way and there was no understanding. The dream bubble she had imagined life would be with Joseph had popped like an overinflated balloon. She had no idea how to refill it.

11
Bonds of Friendship

It was a few weeks since Ripley had been admitted into the hospital. Ms. Wilks and Lauren had spent about a week visiting with Ripley before they headed back home to arrange for Ripley to live at the British Columbia rehabilitation centre in Prince George.

Roseway visited every day. During this time, she helped Ripley get dressed. She massaged her hands, her neck, and her legs to keep circulation flowing. They did leg lifts and hand exercises, stacking cones and squeezing a little ball. Ripley was often frustrated at the difficultly of trying to do something that once would have been so simple.

Rose bought Ripley a pretty flowered bandana to wear on her head, as her hair wasn't growing back because of the effects of the chemo. Ripley didn't like the bald look and couldn't wait until her hair grew long again. Even bald, she was beautiful.

The day came when Ripley had to leave the Kelowna hospital. They both cried as they said their goodbyes. Ripley knew she would miss Roseway and all the encouragement she gave her every day. She told her just that. "I can't thank you enough for all you have done for me. I feel bad that you didn't go on your honeymoon. I sure appreciated your sacrifice for me. You truly are an example of a friend. You put your life aside for mine. I don't know how I will ever repay you."

If you only knew the half of it, Roseway thought. *I wish I could tell you how bad things are between Joseph and me at this time.* She didn't want to burden her friend with her problems, so she put on her pretend face and teased Ripley. "Now who is being the mushy one? Ripley, you don't have to repay me. That is what friends are for. We will keep in touch. Phone me if there is anything you need."

"I sure will. You do the same. What will you do when I leave?"

"I'm not sure. Maybe I'll take that botany class at the college. I'll give Joseph more of my time. There is a lot of work to do around that old farmhouse. Don't worry, I'll keep busy."

"Well, it looks like the shuttle bus is here. Can you wheel me aboard?"

"I sure can, pal."

Roseway helped Ripley onto the bus and got her all strapped in. With a reluctance to say goodbye, Rose hugged Ripley. Ripley rested her head on Rose's shoulder like a baby in a cradle. Ripley wanted to cry in the comfort she felt. Instead she bit her quivering lip and asked Rose if she could do her one more thing. "Could you scratch my nose one more time?"

They both laughed.

Roseway wiped the moisture from her friend's eye. "See you, pal." Then she walked off the bus and they waved goodbye through the window as the bus pulled away.

Ripley was put into a rehabilitation program. Ripley's boyfriend, Professor JD, came and worked with Ripley to try to help her regain the feeling in her arms and legs by doing many exercises. It just wasn't the same working with JD as it was with Rose. JD had great hopes that Ripley would recover quickly. He was always serious and didn't make the therapy fun.

As each day passed, he was disheartened to see little change. His visits gradually became fewer and fewer, until he stopped visiting altogether. Ripley felt the void of not having him there. Somehow, she understood why he stopped visiting. Part of her didn't want him to feel chained to her. In her physical condition, she had many mixed emotions about having a relationship with him.

Ms. Wilks visited every other day for the first month, and then her visits changed to once a week. It seemed that people just wanted to see her get up and walk, and for things to be the way they were, but it just wasn't happening. The therapy was draining and Ripley was feeling lonely. Roseway was too far away to visit, living near Kelowna. Ripley began to realize the limitations of her disability. The peace she had initially been feeling seemed to dwindle. She felt sick from the chemo. *God, I thought I was going to help other people. How can I help anyone in this condition? I can't even feed myself.*

HAVE PATIENCE, MY BELOVED. MY TIMING IS PERFECT.

Depression began to cover her like a dark cloud. The excitement she felt from her experience and her motivation was fading. Even when Ms. Wilks did come to visit, Ripley didn't even want to get out of bed.

One day, a young woman walked down the long hall. She was using crutches. With difficulty, she tried to open the door to Ripley's room. Her crutches banged against the door.

Ripley yelled from under her blankets, "Do you have to make such a racket?"

The woman stood quietly for a moment at the foot of Ripley's bed. Ripley lay in her bed with the pillow over her head. The girl took one of her metal crutches and banged it on the sidebar of the bed.

"Why don't you get your lazy but out of that bed? It is a beautiful day. Don't just lay there like a bump on a log feeling sorry for yourself. There is a big world out there waiting for Ripley Wilks."

The voice sounded very familiar. *It couldn't be,* Ripley thought, afraid to remove the pillow and look.

The woman put a little flower on the table. "Here, I brought you a flower."

Ripley slowly pulled her head out from under the pillow. Her eyes opened wide with surprise. "Oh my God, Abby, is it really you? I can't believe it!"

"Yes, it is me. Long time no see. How are you doing, kiddo? I saw the article in the newspaper about you. Well, I had to come and make sure you are doing alright. As you can see from my crutches, I've had to cope with a little rehabilitation myself. I haven't regained the proper use of my legs yet. I'm somewhat disabled now."

"Abby, I can't believe it is you. I'm so happy to see you. Praise God. You won't believe this ... it is a long story—I know about your accident. I didn't know when it happened. God showed me in a vision that you ... had an accident when you left the brownstone that day. He showed me your rehab and everything. I would have liked to have been there for you, but I was on the street and didn't read newspapers. It is so nice to see you again. I can't believe it. Will you give me a hug?"

Abby sat on the side of her bed, leaned the crutches against the wall, and reached down and lifted Ripley's limp body up off the bed and gave her a hug. Ripley's arms hung limp. She wanted so much to hug her old friend back. Tears streamed down both their faces.

Abby asked, "Did you say God showed you a vision about me? I didn't know you believed in God. When did this happen?"

"Well, when you asked me to leave the brownstone, I lived on the street for the next year. I met this girl named Roseway; she reminded me of you. She had that same belief in God. Some things happened, and through it all, I came to know Christ as my Saviour. Anyway, my friend got married and at her wedding, the tumour that was in my brain started to bleed and I collapsed and ended up in a coma. When I was in the coma, I found myself transported to another place. I believe it was heaven. God showed me many visions of my life. One of the visions was of you and me. God showed me what we did. He also showed me what happened that day, after you left. I saw your accident as if I was standing right there on the sidewalk. He showed me a vision of you in rehabilitation, trying to learn how to walk again. Abby, God does forgive the sin we commit when we repent. He showed me that I had to learn to love myself the way He loves me. It is a pure love. It is a love of acceptance. Not to accept the sin, but love the sinner."

Abby sat quiet and speechless for a moment, then exclaimed, "Praise God. That is so awesome. I struggled with regret. It was hard to forgive myself. I felt so ashamed, couldn't accept God's love or forgiveness for a long time. It felt like I committed the worst of sins. Even church people made me feel guilty when I tried to talk to them for help. Some rejected me when I told my testimony. This only made me feel more condemnation. Then one day it was like a light came on in my head. I realized that Jesus took that sin upon him when he died on the cross. He removed it as far as the east is from the west. For so long I carried that guilt with me. That day I realized I had to give it all to God. For a long time, I thought my accident was my punishment for what we did. Then God showed me there is a bigger purpose in all things. God also showed me that it is okay to love you and other women as one would love a sister. I know that anything more is not what I am comfortable with or the right choice for me. There is such a freedom to live knowing this to be true. I'm here to be your friend again. I want to help you with your rehabilitation. Can we put the past behind us? Will you be my friend again?"

Ripley smiled. "There is no reason why we can't be wonderful friends. We have both matured and changed in many ways in the last few years."

12
Voices of Doubt

It had been a bumpy road since the wedding day. The constant guilt and verbal jabs created an invisible wall between Roseway and Joseph. She was pulling away from him slowly, to protect her heart. Joseph only made himself feel even more insignificant, not realizing he was part of the problem. His way of coping was to keep busy working, going on trips. Ignoring the problem seemed to whitewash it.

The alarm clock went off at 4 a.m. with the loud sound of the rooster call. Joseph made himself a thermos of coffee for the road. Roseway got up and made him some sandwiches to take with him. The last couple of months had taken their toll on the relationship. They were more like ships that pass in the night than they were newlyweds. Dressed in her yellow housecoat, Roseway rubbed her eyes to remove the sleepiness. She filled his lunch box with food and walked to the door with him.

"Have a safe trip. Be careful," Roseway whispered in his ear as if it was part of the routine.

Joseph brushed back his black hair with his hands, took the lunch box from her and kissed her on the forehead. Roseway hugged him and kissed him on the lips. "When will you be back?"

She asked with an underlying tone that said, "How long will you be gone this time?"

Trying to appease the sad expression on her face, he responded, "Hopefully it will only take five days to go to Oregon and back. I should be home Saturday if everything co-operates. The weather conditions are supposed to be good. We know how quick that can change when riding through the mountains. I'll call you when I get to Oregon."

They gave each other one more little kiss before he went out the door and drove away in his truck. His little kiss left her feeling like she wanted more of that old passion they once shared not so long ago. Roseway felt tired and somewhat depressed. It was so early in the morning. She managed to find only a little motivation to walk back to her bedroom and tuck herself firmly and securely under the warm blankets. Her eyes closed as soon as her head hit the pillow.

Pellets of hail hit the windows like they were being fired from a shotgun. Darkness invaded the room like death. The wind howled like a pack of wolves. Hail and snow swirled around and around in circular motions, hitting the outside walls of the house. The wind looked like mini tornados desperately trying to find a crack to enter the farmhouse. Roseway walked out from her bedroom, frightened by the noises. A feeling of loneliness walked beside her. The old farm floorboards creaked under her feet with each step.

Entering the dining room, she was surprised to see Doubt sitting at the head of the dining room table. She was not alone. Doubt had brought some relatives. They all stared at Roseway like they were old-time friends waiting for a big welcome home party. Doubt was the ring leader and encouraged Roseway to sit at the table with them. Doubt grabbed Roseway by the hand and pulled her toward the table.

"Here, this chair is for you. Please sit here beside me. I'll keep you company. I know that you are all alone again. There is no one else here with you in

this big old farmhouse. Everyone else is off living their own lives and you are not a part of their lives anymore. It's not really that much different than living in that old cabin with Big Joe, now is it?"

Roseway's face took on a forlorn expression to think that to be true.

Doubt continued. "I believe you know my brother, Melancholy. The two of you have known each other since childhood."

Melancholy greeted her. "Yes Rose, I have missed you. I have not had a visit from you for a long time. We spent so much time in that valley of despair by that old cabin when you were younger. Now I can see that things are not going so good for you at this time. You must be very tired and sad. I'll be your friend again, since you are feeling lonely. Do you remember my brother, Misery? He is here, too."

Misery spoke with a baritone voice. "Hello, Rose. It has been too long since our last visit. You know the saying, 'Misery enjoys company.' So, I thought I'd make the trip over. After all, I have enjoyed your company many times."

Roseway looked around the table. There were two others sitting close beside her. One had a crimson-looking face, aged and miserable from years of being angry. His name was Fury.

The other was tapping the table incessantly, as if to say hurry up so I can introduce myself. Finally, he interrupted Misery. "Hello Roseway, surely you remember me, Impatience. You can call me Imp for short. I'm your friend who always prodded you to get things done now and not later. If it wasn't for me, you would still be sitting in that old log cabin with Big Joe."

A rough voice spoke up loudly. "Rose, don't listen to these nincompoops. They rattle on incessantly and pull you astray. Don't listen to them or anyone else. Just do your own thing, let out all that frustration. Blast them all, Rose. Listen to your uncle Fury."

Doubt piped up, "Who invited you to this table, Fury?"

"I invited myself. Rose needs someone here to protect her."

Roseway sat around the table with all her friends, listening to their comments back and forth to one another. Then she raised her voice above them all.

"All of you be quiet. I never invited you to sit at my table or even enter into my house."

Fury applauded. "That is my girl—get angry and tell them off."

Roseway snapped her head around like it was on a swivel. "That includes you, Fury."She moved on to the next. "Doubt, you are like a gnawing termite eating away at human flesh. You are not my friend, never was, never will be. You can be the first to leave. I'm sick of listening to you and your whiney voice. Get out, now."

Like a snowball rolling downhill, her words were unstoppable. "Melancholy, I can relate to you. That soft, sorrow-filled voice can almost seem comforting at times. Your sad tone can almost draw me in, being the melancholic personality that I am. I could easily imagine myself tucked away in some beautiful garden with you, feeling sorry for myself. That is not a place I want to be anymore. That was a different time and place. I'm stronger now. Life has changed. I've changed. I must ask you to leave also.

"Misery, if you want company so much, then go with Doubt. She could use a little misery.

"Finally, as for you Impatience, I have a new friend and her name is Patience. I find her to be much more helpful than you. All your prodding and pushing only causes me to make rash decisions that put me and other people at risk. Out you go with the others. None of you are welcome here anymore. Get out, get out! Close the door behind you."

One by one, they all left the room. Alone, Roseway sat at the table, smiling like the mouse that ate the cheese. The room was quiet. The storm door swung back and forth, banging against the house as the wind continued to blow hard. The door banged and banged and banged.

Roseway was startled by the sound and awoke from her dream.

She was so tired from being deep in sleep. Perhaps God was trying to tell her that she had the boldness and authority in life to come against the lies of the devil. All she had to do was realize the authority she has in Christ Jesus.

The door continued to bang. Groggily, Roseway shuffled her feet along the floor while putting her housecoat back on. She went to the door to see what was banging. There stood her neighbour, Camay, holding a little box of cookies in her hand while banging on the door.

"Hello, Camay. Please come in. I have not seen you for a while. Things have been quite hectic around here since the wedding."

"I heard what happened to your friend at the wedding. That is terrible. Word spreads fast in this neck of the woods. I hope you don't mind me dropping by unexpected. I noticed Joseph's truck was gone, so I thought maybe you would like a little company. How about we have a cup of tea to go with this box of goodies?"

"Sure, please come in out of the cold. What do you have in the box?" Roseway lifted the lid to peek. Smelling the fragrance of the baked cookies, she rubbed her tummy. "Hmm, they look delicious."

"I did a lot of baking over the holidays, so I thought I would bring you a variety of home-baked cookies. My three children are visiting. Today, they are taking advantage of the ski hill at Big White. They are spending the day on the mountain."

Roseway filled the old cast iron kettle with water and put it on the wood stove to boil. "Oh, that's right, you have three children. What are their names?"

Smiling proudly, Camay described her children. "Nathan is the oldest. He is twenty-four. He works as a graphic designer for a marketing company in Toronto. Samson is twenty-three, just a couple years older than you. He went to college and studied to be an electrician. Now he is working as an apprentice in that field.

My youngest is Nicole. Currently she is enrolled in a veterinarian school. It is so nice to have them visiting. We don't get to see each other very often, being that we live so far apart.

"They went through a difficult time when their father and I divorced. They couldn't believe their perfect family fell apart. Thus they also had to cope with many changes in their lives. I'm enjoying having them again. It almost feels like old times having them home again. I'll hate to see them leave. Goodbyes always make me feel sad."

The whistle blew as steam flew from the kettle's spout. Roseway made a nice pot of tea. Camay dunked her shortbread cookie into her tea as they continued to talk. "It must be a little scary to stay in this big house by yourself when your husband is away. Does it bother you at all?"

"I don't enjoy when Joseph goes away because I miss him. However, I'm accustomed to being alone. At least the house is warm and somewhat protected from animals and such. If I would only remember to lock the door, it would be safer. This house is too big at times. It is so much bigger than the old one-room cabin I grew up in. In that way, yes, it can feel a little strange to me at times."

"Did you enjoy your honeymoon?"

"Oh, that is sore subject around here. No, we didn't go on a honeymoon because Ripley took sick. I couldn't stand the thought of leaving her when she was in such bad condition. Joseph didn't understand, so we have spent most of the time since we married not talking to one another. It is so hard. I really wanted to go on the honeymoon and please Joseph, but at the same time I felt being here for Ripley was more important than us. Maybe I was wrong. That is the way I looked at the situation. Because we didn`t go, I saw a different side of Joseph that I had not known existed. That does bother me somewhat. He kind of pulled away from me because he has been so angry with me. Oh, there I go again talking too much. You don't need to hear my little problems. I imagine they will eventually work themselves out. I hope so."

"My advice, dear, is to fix the problems right away. Biggest mistake is to ignore the problems and let them fester. They eventually explode in your face. The bible gives some good advice about that. It says something about not depriving each other except by mutual consent and for a time. Satan loves to tempt us humans in our weaknesses. I'm talking from experience. My relationship with my husband went downhill when we stopped communicating. My husband ended up having an affair. "

"That wouldn't happen with us. Joseph would never be unfaithful."

"I would hope not, but our body sometimes reacts in ways it should not. Temptation is around every corner, ready to pounce when we least expect it. Circumstances can cause us to lose control of all rational thinking. The devil is always waiting for an opportunity to kill, steal and destroy. Oh, will you look at the time. I best get back and cook some dinner. The children will be starving after a full day of skiing. Hey, why don't you come over for dinner tonight? You can meet my kids."

Roseway thought for a second, and then accepted the offer. "That is very nice of you. Hey, why not? I'd just be here by myself anyway. Okay."

Camay put her coat on and then leaned against the wall while she put on her fur boots. "How does six o'clock sound?"

Roseway confirmed with a smile. "See you then."

13
Burning Ring of Fire

Roseway dressed in a warm white sweater and black pants. She walked the quarter mile to Camay's house. When she arrived, Camay took her coat and introduced her to each of her grown children. Then they sat in front of the warm fireplace in the living room and had a glass of wine before dinner.

Nathan was very artistic. He was working on his laptop most of the time during Rose`s visit, only lifting his head periodically when a topic of interest came up. He was a quiet young man with introspective thoughts, studious and gifted with an extraordinary artistic expression.

Samson was a little more conversational. One could see he liked attention and was quite the storyteller. Perhaps he inherited his mother`s flair for turning non-fiction into fiction by embellishing his stories with a lot of exaggeration. He also took a liking to Rose. Once or twice, Rose caught a look in his eyes that sent a few vibes her way. At dinner, his foot touched hers under the table a couple of times. Rose felt the connection and tried to ignore it. Samson had a strong physique and a magnetic personality. He was smooth when it came to attracting women. Perhaps it was the brash confidence and charisma he wore like it was a fine leather jacket.

When Nicole could find a break in the conversation, she asked Rose to tell some of her stories of when she lived off the land. Nicole found them quite intriguing. Nicole's nature was to always preserve the lives of animals whenever possible. She thought the story Rose told about killing a bear showed an amazing act of courage by both Rose and her dog Icon.

When Rose told her story, she couldn't help but glance at Samson, who never broke eye contact. His eyes followed her movements. He watched her lips move as if every word she spoke exuded pleasure to him. Rose felt somewhat aroused by the attention she was getting from him. She tried to shut out Samson's flirtations, but it did feel good. *I can't allow myself to have these feelings toward him. I`m married to Joseph. I have to stop looking at him.*

The night continued, and they took their tea into the family room where they played a game of Trivial Pursuit. They laughed throughout the entire game. Even though Rose bombed in the game, she enjoyed the relaxation and laughter. It felt good for a change, in comparison to all the tension she had felt over the past months. She didn't know much trivia, as she lived such a sheltered life for so many years.

The game took a long time to play, and it was getting late. Rose thanked Camay for the wonderful evening and a delicious dinner, saying that she should go home. Samson volunteered to drive her. Roseway said she could walk. Camay refused that idea. "It is too dark and too far to walk by yourself in the dark. Samson will drive you home. That won`t be a problem."

Samson went outside and started up his mother's spacious Chevy and turned on the heat to defog the windows. After Rose finished her goodbyes she went out to the car. Samson drove the car out of the driveway. The moonlight shined on his blond hair and onto his face, enhancing the whiteness of his teeth as he smiled.

He broke the silence. "If I may tell you, Rose, I think you are the most beautiful woman I`ve ever seen. I can`t believe your husband would leave you here all by yourself. If you were my wife, I`d never leave you alone. I would lavish my love on you all the time."

His flattery was appealing to her, as she had been feeling somewhat shunned by Joseph.

Subtly, Samson placed his strong hand over top of hers and caressed it softly with his thumb. It brought Roseway pleasure. *His touch feels nice. Letting him feel my hand can't hurt. Actually, it feels amazing. He is very handsome. I can't believe I'm thinking this.*

Rose couldn`t believe the reaction her body was feeling to the touch. It felt good. Her face blushed, looking like rose petals on her cheeks. She allowed him to continue. Thoughts invaded her mind as Samson stopped the car in her driveway and turned out the lights. *I better get in the house before we do something we shouldn't.*

Samson leaned over her to unlock the door so she could get out of the car. His sweet breath met her sense of smell as he spoke softly. "The automatic locks don't work on this car. Let me get that for you." Leaning over her, his face brushed across hers. He stopped as he smelled the fragrance of her hair. "Hmm, you smell good." He rubbed his face on her, breathing her fragrance.

Before she knew what to do, he kissed her on the cheek. His kiss felt electric. *I can`t do this,* she thought.

His lips met hers and it was like all control was gone. Any rational thoughts disappeared as Roseway was caught in the clutches of physical pleasure. Samson pushed her seat back into a lying position, kissing her all over. They moaned with pleasure. Lustfully, she kissed him back. A river of emotions flowed from her like a fountain. His caresses captured her every emotion as he slowly undressed her, kissing her. Their bodies reacted to one another in pleasure. Her eyes opened wide.

The windows fogged with condensation as he lay on top of her for a moment, catching his breath. The pleasure Rose felt took her breath away as her heart pounded. When she realized what they had done, the pleasure was quickly replaced by guilt as she began to remember Joseph. *Why didn't I stop him?* Her heart was pounding and her mind was racing with questions.

Samson buttoned up Roseway's top while kissing her still. Samson felt exhilarated. "Can I drop by your house again tomorrow? You are incredible. I'd love to see you again," he asked with a longing in his voice.

Without speaking a word of reply, Rose opened the door and stood by the car like she was in a trance. She didn't know what to say in answer. Her desires felt like saying yes, but her conscience was saying no. Slowly, she turned and walked toward the house. Samson yelled out of the car window, "See you tomorrow, Rose. Have a good night`s sleep."

Rose went into her empty house and went into the bathroom to run a hot bath. She stood in front of the mirror, touching her face, expecting some kind of rebuke to jump out at her. There was none. She slipped herself into the bath and soaked in the warm water like it was a comforting blanket. Closing her eyes, she could still feel her heart beating faster than normal. She still felt aroused at the thought. Samson`s face kept creeping into her imagination. *What will I do if he comes back tomorrow?* The thought scared her. However, the conviction of wrong was heavy in her heart for she knew she had sinned against God, Joseph and even her own body.

Dressed in her nightgown, she kneeled at her bedside and cried as she prayed, *Father God, please forgive me for the sin I committed tonight. I don`t know what else to pray but to ask for your forgiveness. Lead me Lord not into temptation and deliver me from evil. The heart is willing but the flesh is weak. Your power is more victorious than the temptations of the heart. Create in me a clean heart, God. I pray in Jesus' name.*

14
Road Trip

Joseph was nicely on his way. He liked driving the transport across the countryside. There was something peaceful about the journey. His favourite music played. The long trip gave him a lot of time to think, reflect and talk to God. *I can't believe I'm taking this trip. It is not exactly what I had planned. But then again, my plans are not always your plans. I felt I had to take this job to get me out of the house before I said something really hurtful to Rose. She just disappointed me so much by not wanting to go on the honeymoon. I love her so much that I just wanted to share that time together in some romantic place. Maybe I'm too much of a dreamer. It was just bad timing. It is not that I don't care about Ripley's condition, I do care. Perhaps I am just being a little selfish, a little hard on Rose even. She has been through so much in her young life. I just wanted to give her a really special time. It felt like she took that away from us. For whatever reason, the honeymoon didn't happen. God, I don't know how to break through this feeling I've had toward Rose. I lost focus. Forgive me, God, for behaving like such a jerk. I've been acting like a stubborn fool. She wants to be loved and I know that I haven't been showing love to her in the way I should be. I pray, God, that somehow we will get back to the way we were with one another. Restore that passion between us. Now I'm a couple hundred miles from home and I miss her so much that I can't wait to get back to her. Protect her, Lord, while I'm away. How can I make it up to her when I get home? How do I get rid of my stupid pride? I didn't expect that married life would be so complicated so soon. Not exactly the nicest way to start a marriage. Help us, Lord, to love each other in the way you have ordained us to love. Please help us, Lord, to gain a right perspective again. When I get back home, I'm going to try and make it up to her. We need your help, Lord.*

Joseph drove mile after mile, dreaming of being back home and in Roseway's arms. When he got to a town he phoned home, but there was no answer.

15
Heap of Trouble

All day, Roseway kept busy working outside, cleaning out the stalls, feeding the chickens and cows. More than anything, she just wanted to keep her mind occupied so she wouldn't think about what happened the night before.

When she finished doing all she could do, she went into the house to shower. Showering under the hot water made her feel cleansed as she watched the dirt fall off of her and disappear down the drain. *Could my sins be washed away so easily?* Rose's guilt was weighing heavily on her heart.

A noise came from the kitchen. It sounded like the squeaky hinge of the door opening. Rose turned off the shower and dried herself, then put on her bathrobe. Cautiously, she walked toward the kitchen calling out, "Is that you, Joseph?"

All of a sudden, she felt his manly body up against her backside. Putting his hands over her eyes, he kissed her behind her ear and down her neck. It felt so good to feel his touch. Her body was aroused. Then he turned her around and kissed her lips. Recognizing the kiss to be Samson, Roseway opened her eyes. Instantaneously, she pulled back. "What do you think you are doing?"

"Last night was incredible. You know it and I know it. I thought we could get together one more time before I head back to Ontario. Maybe you could come with me."

Swallowing the lump in her throat, she stood there feeling so vulnerable, naked under her robe. "You have got to be kidding. Last night should not have happened." She could feel her heart pound in her chest. His kiss moments ago made her lips numb. "I ... don't think that is a good idea," she stuttered breathlessly.

Samson put his finger up to her lips, "Hush, it's okay. You know as well as I know just how great we are together. You can't deny how I make you feel, just like I can't deny how you make me feel. I've been attracted to you since the first moment I laid eyes on you. You didn't know this, but I saw you and Joseph kissing in this kitchen. I saw the way he treated you, how he rejected your love. He is a fool. It didn't look to me like he loves you the way you ought to be loved." Samson kissed her fervently, several times.

The words he spoke to her fuelled her desires. His kisses were passionate, erotic and consuming. She tried to speak through her breathlessness, questioning him as to confirm what he saw that night. "Was that you I saw go passed the window that night?"

"Yes, it was, Rose. I find you so attractive." He slowly nudged her toward the table, continuing to kiss her body. "Yes, I must admit it was me. Mother asked me to come up and borrow some sugar from you. Speaking of sugar, you are like sugar, Roseway, sweet to my taste." He could feel the warmth of her skin on his lips. It made his loins burn with desire. He could hardly speak to finish his story. "When I looked in the window, I didn't want to interrupt, so I watched. I was mesmerised by your beauty." He removed his clothing as he recalled how she looked, and continued to love on her. Rose was saying no with her mouth, but her body was saying yes, responding to his kisses and his touch.

Roseway was fighting within herself. Camay's words of warning rang loud in her ears. *Our body sometimes reacts in ways it should not.* He kissed her lips, locked in desire. Just as Roseway gave herself over to Samson's advances, a knock pounded on the door. Then it flung open.

There stood Camay, reacting out of surprise. All the anger Camay had pushed down from her past flared up like a shaken soda. She was enraged to find her son caught in an adulterous affair. He was behaving like his father. The disappointment ran deep to her soul. "Samson, what in the world do you think you are doing?" Angry, Camay pulled Samson away from Roseway and yelled at him, "Get your clothes back on and get in the car, now!" Samson ran out of the house like it was on fire, doing his pants up as he ran.

Standing there in front of Roseway, Camay reached toward her and did up her robe, pulling it tight around her. "Roseway, you are a married woman. What has got into you? How are you ever going to face Joseph when he returns? My girl, you have gotten yourself into a heap of trouble."

"Camay, please calm down. I know this doesn't look good. Please don't say anything to Joseph. I have to think about how I'm going to tell him what happened. I don't know what came over me. I know it was wrong. Never in my imagination did I think I would have such little control. I'm sorry."

"You don't have to tell me you are sorry. It would be better if you repented to God and to Joseph. I'll give you a couple of weeks to tell him or I will tell him. I know what it is like to live with a person who is unfaithful. It is such a terrible lie and betrayal. I feel somewhat responsible for what my son has done. Remember, Rose, that the truth shall always uncover the lie. The truth will set you free. I'm so disappointed in you and in Samson. I'm sure God is, too.

You can be assured that my son will not step foot on this property again. Please stay away from him, too."

Camay ran out of the house, slamming the door behind her. Rose just collapsed to her knees and wept for hours, just lying on the floor like a defeated soldier. *Oh God, what did I just do? I did it again. What is the matter with me? I can never face Joseph.*

The phone rang and rang. She hesitated to answer it for fear it was Joseph. Finally, Rose couldn't stand it ringing anymore. Feeling very weak from crying, she slowly reached for the phone. Her voice was hoarse from the strain. Quietly, she whispered, "Hello."

The voice on the other end spoke with concern, "Rose, is that you?"

"Yes, it is me," she told Joseph sheepishly.

"What is wrong? You sound like you have been crying. I've been trying to call you. I called last night and didn't get an answer. Then I called again today and no answer. Is everything okay?"

"Yes, Joseph, everything is fine." *I'm not fine. I'm anything but fine.* "I was invited to dinner at the neighbour's house last night. I guess today when you called I was out with the animals, cleaning the stalls."

"You sound different."

"Oh, maybe I'm coming down with a cold or something. My throat is a little scratchy." *I can't tell him the truth.*

"Well, I'm coming home sooner than expected. My truck had a breakdown. So I had to get the company to pick it up to get it fixed. I'm catching a ride back with John. He drives for Transport for Christ, too. I should arrive home some time tonight."

Rose rubbed her hand over her tingling face, feeling unprepared to face him. She tried to sound excited. "That is great news, honey. I can't wait to see you." *I can't face him. How will I ever face him again?*

"Alright then, I'm on a payphone so I better go. Keep the bed warm until I get home."

Roseway heard the dial tone on the other end of the phone as he hung up. Overwhelmed, she screamed in frustrated anger, slamming the phone down again and again, shattering it. That is how she felt deep inside; like her life was in a shambles.

16
Father of Lies

Starting to cry again, Roseway heard a voice taunt her. "Well...well, didn't I tell you?" Doubt laughed. "Swell job, Rose. Joseph will never forgive you. You might as well have filed for divorce already. I guess the apple doesn't fall too far from the tree. Big Joe was evil. Being that he was your father, you are evil, too. What are you going to do, Rose? Are you going to tell lies for the rest of your life? Everyone will know that the good little Christian girl is really a bad girl. All the respect people had for you will soon be forgotten. Being that you are like Big Joe, maybe you could do what he did to solve his problems. At least in the end he showed his love to you. Maybe you could show your love to Joseph the same way? Set him free. Joseph is a good, Godly man. He sure didn't deserve what you did behind his back. That is not love. I don't think you love him at all, or you wouldn't have been so selfish with your desires."

"That is not true. I do love Joseph. I love him more than anything."

"He won't love you anymore, not after you break his heart. When he finds out, he will be shattered. Then again you could save him from ever finding out the truth."

"How ... how can I do that?"

Much like Satan uses scripture to deceive people, Doubt continued to persuade Roseway. "Simple—lay down your life for his life. Jesus even says: 'Greater love has no one than this, that one lay down their life for another.' Sure, he will miss you for a little while. In the long run, he can devote his life to a woman who is faithful to him."

"Why should I listen to you?"

"Rose, Rose, you know I've always been right. My doubts are your doubts. Do what you think is best. You better make up your mind soon. He will be home soon. Remember, you can't face him."

Doubt sat quietly in the chair. Roseway dragged herself into the bathroom, where she filled the tub again with warm water. She slipped herself into the bath and scrubbed her body hard, trying to wash away the sin. She felt so warm in the water that she wished she could just fall deep into it and sleep away forever.

As if Doubt knew what Rose was thinking, she said, "You could sleep forever. It is as simple as taking that razor and cutting your wrist. No more pain, confusion, no more secrets, they all go with you."

One of Joseph's razors sat on the edge of the tub. While removing the blade from the razor, she cut her finger. Watching the blood flow down her finger and drip into the water, she felt like she was in a hypnotic daze. With one slice over her wrist, the blood ran into the bathwater. *Sleepy, I feel so tired. Jesus, I'm bathing in blood, my own blood. Jesus, I wish it was your blood because your blood sanctifies, your blood is redeeming. Jesus, take me home to be with you. Take ... me .... ho—....* Roseway drifted into oblivion.

Joseph entered the house looking for Roseway. "Honey, I'm home." He searched each room in the house until he found her in the bathroom, lying in the tub, her arm hanging limp as her life seeped from the wound on her wrist.

Joseph stood staring into the bloody water. Looking at her white pale skin sent a rush of terror down his legs. For a moment he stood like a frozen statue. Then he cried aloud, "Oh my God, Jesus, help us!" He instinctively grabbed a towel and ripped a piece off of it, then tied it snugly around the wound to stop the bleeding. He took her from the tub of still-warm water and wrapped her tightly in a blanket. Immediately he ran to the phone to dial 911. He noticed the phone was broken into pieces. Then he ran up the stairs to check the other phone and make the call. After, he sat holding her close, rocking her back and forth and praying while he waited for the ambulance to arrive.

The ambulance took ten minutes to get there. Roseway was so cold. Joseph was afraid he was going to lose her, as her heartbeat was very faint. He slapped her face to awaken her. She awoke for a moment, mumbling gibberish. When the ambulance arrived, they took her to the hospital and Joseph went with her. The first thing the paramedics did was give her an intravenous. They stabilized her blood pressure on the way to the hospital.

When Joseph arrived at the hospital, he called Rose's mother Noreen to tell her what happened. "Noreen, Rose is in the hospital. She tried to commit suicide. I don't understand why she did this. She will be okay physically. The doctors have her resting for now. She is in psychiatrics. They are not allowing visitors for the next forty-eight hours. They said they need time to assess her mental state. I just don't get it."

Concerned, Noreen tried to process what she was hearing. "Did you have a fight or something?"

"Well, we have had some disagreements. I don't think they were so bad as to cause her to do this."

"Have you talked to anyone else? Did she leave a note or some clue?"

"No, I haven't talked to anyone. There is no note, nothing. I talked to Rose in the afternoon and she said that she had dinner at Camay's house yesterday. Come to think of it, she has been a little paranoid lately. I caught her talking to herself a couple of times. When I asked her who she was talking to, she just evaded the question and talked about something else."

Looking for some answers, Noreen suggested, "Why don't you come by my house and pick me up? We will take a drive to Camay's house and question her."

There was nothing Joseph could do at the hospital. They would not allow him to visit Rose yet. He was just so relieved that she had survived. It looked like she lost a lot of blood. He wanted to find some answers, but was he prepared for the answers he would receive?

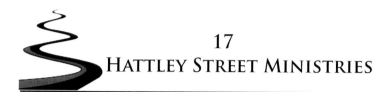

17
Hattley Street Ministries

Abby had worked hard with Ripley in therapy. Gradually, the feeling was coming back into Ripley's hands. Abby was very patient as she helped Ripley play one key of the piano at a time. While the progress was slow and sometimes frustrating for both of them, this helped with the movements of her fingers while the worship songs they sung ministered to their spirit.

They spent a lot of time working together. During that time, Ripley told Abby about each of the visions she had from God. Abby thought they were so meaningful and that God had a great purpose in revealing these things to Ripley. It was very exciting to see what God was doing even in the mist of such a tragedy.

Ripley was about to be let out of the hospital with the condition that she continue therapy every day. Since Abby seemed to be like the oars in a boat that kept Ripley moving forward, it only seemed right to both of them that Ripley move in with Abby. That way they could continue their therapy together. God had truly done a miracle in their relationship. Though they were crippled in physical ways because of their disabilities, they were free in so many other ways. There was no hidden agenda between them. The homosexual tendency they once shared was completely taken away along with the associated guilt. They gained a Godly friendship with one another. This was a season of healing—physically, emotionally and spiritually. God was truly the rudder steering their boat. They moved back to the brownstone where Abby still lived.

It seemed like a lot of time had passed since the first time that Ripley lived there. So much water had run under the bridge. She was a confused, broken teenager of seventeen then. Now she felt like a woman way beyond her twenty-three years. They said wisdom comes with age, or does age come with experience? Perhaps they are both correct. Ripley often thought about the visions she had experienced in what could have been her dying moments. It was just the opposite. In those dying moments, she had really come alive. Now she was living back in the brownstone that once was the abode of brokenness. God had restored what once had been destroyed by false perceptions. A friendship that had seemed destined to fail was now destined for success. Sin of the past had been washed away as far as the east is from the west. That was a new revelation to Ripley, and it awed her to the depth of who she had become.

When Abby had her accident, she had to close up her music business due to her rehabilitation. Then she lived on disability pay, to pay her rent. Now, Abby felt the freedom and a renewed desire to start up her music business again. She put some advertisements in the paper and around town to get things going. More than ever, she wanted to use her music talents to glorify God. Songs poured out onto the pages. Abby and Ripley sang together every day.

One day, they received a phone call. Abby didn't say much as she listened to the person on the other end of the phone. "Yes, okay, sure. When? Alright, we will be there. Okay. Thank you. Talk to you soon. Bye for now."

Ripley asked, "What was that all about?"

Abby dropped her crutches and tried to jump up and down with excitement. "I sent that tape you and I made to Hattley Street Ministries. They want us to come on their show and sing. Not only that, they want us to give our testimony."

Ripley sat shocked. "Really?"

"Yes, we are going to be on television. Have you ever watched the show? Millions of people watch this show."

They both looked at each other and screamed with joy. Out of the blue, Ripley declared, "I have to go shopping. I need to get something nice to wear, something that is pretty and takes the focal point away from this hair. Maybe I'll buy a nice dress. Do you think I could sit on a couch or a chair instead of in this wheelchair?

"I don't see why not."

"When is this awesome, once-in-a-lifetime interview going to take place?"

"That is the scary part ... We only have two weeks to practice our songs and write out our testimony."

"Two weeks? Oh, this is so exciting. Isn't God amazing?"

"He sure is."

Startled by the ringing of the phone, they both gasped, wondering if that was Hattley Street calling them back to cancel. Abby picked up the phone, listened to the person on the other end of the phone for a moment and then passed the phone over to Ripley. Abby's expression scared Ripley, making her wonder what was wrong. Ms. Wilks had spoken to Noreen and heard the news that Rose was in the hospital and had attempted suicide. Ripley hung up the phone and looked at Abby in a way she had never looked before.

"What happened to your friend Roseway? Your mother only told me that she needed to tell you something about her?"

"I can't believe it. Rose tried to kill herself. That is not like her at all. When her father committed suicide, Rose said that he took the coward's way out. We often say one thing, but if we get forced into a situation, we might do another. Roseway always had to be brave. Some of the things she has had to face are incredible. Deep down, she has always been fighting to free this little girl trapped inside of her. I believe that Rose is very sensitive, vulnerable and a scared young lady. She must be really messed up in the head to do that. I was afraid she couldn't handle getting married. I don't think she really dealt with many things from her past. She was kidnapped for twelve years by her psycho dad BJ. He was a bad dude. Partly the reason I'm in this chair today.

"Should I go to her? Rose never left my side the entire time I was in the Kelowna hospital. For the last few years, she has been my closest friend. I owe her so much. I don't know what to do. I just got back, and the rehabilitation is finally showing some progress, and then we have this television show in two weeks. What do I do?"

"You could go, but Hattley Street is a great opportunity that we have been given. You are barely out of rehabilitation. I don't think it would be good for your health to be travelling back there so soon. Hey, it is up to you. Why don't you pray about it? Ask God what he wants you to do. I would imagine Rose is getting psychiatric help at the hospital. Is there much you can do to help her while she is in hospital? Maybe it would be more helpful to Rose if you visited her when she gets out? Doing this show is such a great way to glorify God. It's a tough decision to make. I'm sure you will know in your heart which one to choose. I'm sure you will know the best time to go if we pray.

"Heavenly Father, we are so thankful for this opportunity to give our testimonies to glorify you for all you do, for who you are in our lives. We pray for Roseway at this time and ask you to bring your emotional healing to her. Protect her from the lies of the enemy. Also, could you please give Ripley an assurance that can only come from you? Help Ripley to know what you want her to do. We give thanks, knowing that you, God, are in control of all things. Amen."

Abby left the decision to Ripley. Two weeks later, they sat on a couch on the set of Hattley Street Ministries. Ripley was dressed in a pretty yellow-flowered dress that flowed down over her legs. Through the eyes of the man behind the camera, he would not know from looking at Ripley that she had a disability. She looked like an angel, wearing a matching yellow scarf around her head. Their testimony was powerful and moving. Pastor Ken Hattley asked them questions. With honesty and humility, they shared their story. They closed off the show with a song from their recording. Their voices harmonized to perfect pitch. Many viewers called in for prayer because they could relate to their testimonies. It was reported to them two days later that through that telecast, more than 4,500 souls accepted Christ as their Saviour.

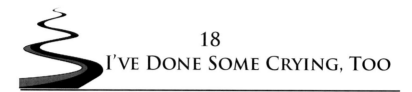

18
I'VE DONE SOME CRYING, TOO

There are many lonely people in the world. Some walk the streets like nomads with no place to go. Other people shut themselves in their homes. Their television set is more like their best friend. Their world is one program or soap opera after another. They search through the channels to find something to break the monotony of their lives. Some are bedridden with sickness. No one visits. They stare at their bedposts. For some, the only human contact they have is when a nurse changes their diaper or rolls them over.

Many people have devoted their lives to their jobs, burying themselves under stacks of paper and deadlines. Others intoxicate themselves with alcohol or prescription drugs. These are the people who called Hattley Street Ministries that night—some with regrets, others with repentance, some people feeling despaired because of the wrongs they have committed. They all had the same thing in common. They were searching for fulfillment, joy, peace, love, healing, hope and forgiveness.

One caller was Amadeus. This man was broken hearted. He was terminal with cancer and was told by doctors that he likely had only a month to live. When he called in to the Hattley phone lines that night, he just wept as he talked to the operator. He told his sad story to this sympathetic stranger on the other end of the line. Amadeus knew he was a sinner. For years, his sin ate away at him more than the cancer. A drunken stupor, a wrong decision, changed his life and the lives of his family forever. There was nothing he could do to change it or take it back. The damage was done.

Sitting on a bar stool that night, the little television set nailed to the corner wall was flipped to the channel where Hattley Street was being aired. Jack, a regular customer, also sat at the bar. His skin was haggard, making him look older than he was. The smell of cigarette smoke lingered from his clothing. With the converter in his hand, he was flipping channels on the television. With his drunken slur, he made loud comments about each show. When the television changed to Hattley Street, the button on the converter seemed to stick.

Jack drew attention to himself and to the show when he noisily announced, "I don't want to watch some religious crap. This converter is broken." He kept pressing the button repeatedly, but it wouldn't change.

When Amadeus looked up at the television, he recognized the angelic face on the screen. His hand came down hard on Jack's hand that was holding the converter. His strong hand almost broke the bones in the drunkard's hand. "Leave the channel right where it is."

He barely recognized the angelic face, for she had matured from a young teen to a beautiful woman. When he heard the woman's name, he just cried. Tears fell into his beer. Amadeus Wilks had not seen or talked to Ripley since that dreadful night eight years earlier. On that sobering night, when Amadeus realized the horrible thing he had done, he left their house and never looked back. He was too ashamed and afraid to look back at the carnage he left behind.

Sitting at the bar that night, he wrote down the Hattley Street hotline number. Broken like a tamed stallion, he made the call. The sympathetic listener gave him hope in Jesus. Amadeus Wilks was only one person of many who called. Perhaps he was caller number two or caller number eight hundred. To God, Amadeus was as important to him as caller number one. In that call to Hattley Street, he accepted Christ as his Saviour and repented his sin. An incredible weight was lifted from his shoulders. With one month to live, there was only one more person he needed to ask for their forgiveness. *If only some way, I could tell Ripley I'm sorry. I've done some crying, too.*

* * *

A loud knock rattled the brownstone door. Ripley wheeled her chair to the door. Thrilled with the news of the results of the show, she was on a holy high. When she answered the door and saw him standing there, her jaw almost hit the floor. She was speechless. Amadeus looked like he had aged twenty years in the eight years he had been out of her life.

Amadeus spoke softly to Ripley. "I was wondering if I could have a moment of your time? There is something I would like to tell you. I wouldn't blame you if you slammed the door in my face. I deserve it."

In that moment, memories flashed like a tidal wave crashing against the shore, reminding her of what he had done to her when she was fifteen. She wanted to close the door. For a moment, she envisioned herself getting up out of the wheelchair and pounding him with her fists. Instead, she went to close the door but changed her mind as an incredible peace flooded the room. She kept remembering what Acacia had said: "Sometimes things are not the way they seem. There is always a bigger picture, God's picture."

Ripley turned around, opened the door and invited her father to come in. "What is it that you would like to say to me?" Her voice was wavering.

Sincerely, he spoke in a soft tone of repentance. "Ripley, I'm so sorry for what I did to you eight years ago. There are no excuses for what I did. There is no reason on earth why I should ever expect that you should forgive me, but I have to ask, will you forgive me?"

Ripley had a flashback of when she was a child. The memory of being raped was fresh in her mind, but other memories reminded her of how much she once loved her dad. She pictured herself sitting on his knee. A smile came to her face. Then she spoke. "Dad, you are half right. There is no reason on earth why I should forgive you. There is every reason in Heaven that tells me I must forgive you. For this reason, I do forgive you."

He broke down and cried like a baby, kneeling at her feet with his head in her lap. She patted the hair on the back of his head, sensing his true repentance.

With a final farewell, he thanked her with a hug. "Thank you, Ripley. I am going on a long journey soon. You will not see me again."

Choking back the tears, she whispered, "I can't explain it, Dad, but I know. I know you are going away. God has told me that you are going home again. He told me to tell you not to be afraid. His grace is sufficient to save. I'll see you before you know it. Dad, there is no clock in heaven."

Amadeus kissed Ripley on the hand and told her how proud he was of her. He turned around to walk out the door, and stopped for a second as if to take one last look at his daughter, clicking one last snapshot in his memory. He waved his hand as his eyes watered, then he said goodbye and walked out the door.

19
Looking for Answers

Camay drew back the curtain and peered through the window when she heard the car doors slam. Noticing it was Joseph and Rose's mother Noreen, her face frowned with questions. *What are they doing here? Where is Roseway? What am I going to say to them?*

They knocked on the door. Camay hesitated to answer. Suitcases were lined up in front of the door, as her children were catching a plane back to Ontario that afternoon. Opening the door, she greeted them with a smile. "Hello, Joseph, and aren't you Roseway's mother? I've seen you from time to time at the diner. Would you like to come in? Don't mind the mess; I'm taking my children to the airport soon. Would you like a tea or coffee?"

Nicole, Samson and Nathan were sitting at the kitchen table finishing up a late breakfast. Joseph and Noreen followed Camay into the kitchen. Camay introduced everyone. While Camay was pouring two more cups of coffee, she asked, "Why didn't you bring Rose with you today?"

There was a pause in the conversation, then Noreen began to speak. "We thought you should know that Rose is in the hospital. I'll just get to the point. Last night she tried to kill herself."

Samson almost choked on his coffee. "Is she alive?" he asked with a concerned expression.

"Yes, she is alive. Thank God. The doctors won't let anyone talk to her yet. We were wondering if any of you talked to her yesterday, or if you noticed anything strange in her behaviour when she was at dinner the other night?"

Camay didn't want to say anything at that moment about Samson and Rose. She had told Roseway she had two weeks to tell Joseph about what happened. With Nathan and Nicole sitting at the table, she did not want a big commotion. Samson just kept looking into his empty cup, spinning it around in his hand nervously. Camay told Joseph and Noreen, "We had a wonderful time at dinner the other night. Roseway seemed to be enjoying herself. Other than that, I can't really say." *I'm not really telling a lie. Besides, what good would it do to bring everything up now?*

Camay continued. "Please let me know when Roseway can have visitors. I would love to go see her. I'm sorry we can't be of any more help to you. Oh my goodness, look at the time. Do you kids have all your things packed and ready to go? We have to be at the airport for check-in by noon." She turned back to Noreen, not looking at Joseph. "I'm sorry to cut your visit short. You know how airports can be. Like I said, please keep me posted. If there is anything else I can do, don't hesitate to let me know. Sorry to hear about Rose. We will have to get together again soon."

Noreen agreed. "Yes, we will do that. Thank you for the coffee and for being such a great neighbour to Rose and Joseph. It is comforting to know that she has someone like you close by if she needs some help."

Joseph and Noreen left, but Joseph was still not satisfied. He didn't know who to blame, so he started to blame himself. "I shouldn't have taken that trip. We never had our honeymoon. I didn't exactly treat her the way I should have. I was ticked off at her and I let her know it. When I phoned her last night, she did seem a little different. I thought she sounded like she had been crying. Rose said she was fine, just had a scratchy throat."

Noreen tried to comfort Joseph. "We will see what the doctors have to say. By tomorrow they should let us visit with her."

During that forty-eight hour period, doctors had stabilized Roseway's blood levels. Noreen and Joseph spoke with the hospital psychologist, Dr. Ross. He tried to give a possible explanation.

"I have exhausted every avenue researching through Rose's hospital records. I studied the notes from the other hospital in Prince George, where Rose had stayed when she had an emotional breakdown a few years ago. The police profile that was done on Rose also shows some interesting unbalances. There was a lot of trauma and upheaval in her entire life. It would seem that something traumatic must have happened recently for her to have felt there was no other way out of the problem. In her mind, she couldn't cope with the ramifications of what happened. It shut her down. We have given her some medication to try and stimulate the brain. Right now, she is just closed off to everything and everyone. She won't talk. We can give it some time to see if she snaps back to reality. Or we can try a form of electric shock. That would be my last choice of action."

"What can we do to help her?" Noreen asked.

"Just be there for her. Talk to her about good memories. Tell her pleasant stories. Show her you love her. You can go in and see her now, but prepare yourself. She is not in a normal state of mind."

Roseway sat in a chair wearing a hospital gown. Her head was drooped down, with her hair fallen down over her face. Joseph gently kneeled down in front of her. He brushed back the hair from her face. He smiled at her with love and concern in his eyes, then kissed her cheek. His smile slowly fell from his face as there was no response from Roseway. She just stared into space like she was someplace else. Her eyes looked empty. “Rose, honey, I’m here. I love you so much. Come back to me, Rose.”

Saliva drooled from her mouth, lethargic from the drugs the doctors had given her. Joseph just wanted to cry, looking at the shell Roseway had become. Overwhelmed, he said to Noreen, “Please excuse me.” He quickly walked out the door and went to the chapel and cried.

Noreen took a brush from her purse and combed Rose’s hair and put it in a ponytail. “Oh, Rose, everything is going to be alright. We have to get you dressed and out of this horrible nightgown that you are wearing.” Noreen walked Roseway to her room and sifted through the drawer beside her bed and pulled out her clothes. Lovingly, she helped Rose dress. “Now, that is much better, isn’t it? You look like yourself again.”

For two weeks, Roseway was in a state of despondency. Joseph and Noreen took turns visiting. Every day before Joseph visited, he went to the chapel and prayed, crying out before God. “How long, oh Lord, must I call for help, but you do not listen? I cry out to you on behalf of Roseway and ask you to break this trapping of her mind. Evil roams the earth trying to kill, steal and destroy that which is good. When, God, will you break Satan’s grip? Please Lord, intervene and bring restoration and health. I love her so much. I would do anything to have her back with a sound mind and body.”

The Lord replied. MY SON JOSEPH, LOOK AND BE AMAZED. I AM GOING TO DO SOMETHING IN YOUR DAYS THAT YOU WOULD NOT BELIEVE, EVEN IF YOU WERE TOLD. (Habakkuk 1:5, NIV)

Every evening, they would take the patients into the sitting room where a small television was playing. The program on the television was Hattley Street Ministries. It was the episode with Ripley and Abby giving their testimony. Roseway sat in the chair and stared at the television without a blink. Ripley and Abby sang their song with a harmonic sound that reached beyond the studio. Pastor Ken Hattley gave his devotional message after the song. He closed with a prayer of forgiveness, making an invitation to the listening audience to accept Christ. He told the audience that the phone lines were open, and if you wanted to talk to someone and pray, to call the number at the bottom of the screen.

With a groan, Roseway forced an ear-splitting roar. The nurse immediately came to Roseway's attention to make sure she was alright. They soon took her back to her room, where she slept for the night. Something in that show had triggered a response. When the doctors made the connection to Roseway's friend Ripley, they wanted to get her to visit Roseway as soon as possible.

Noreen called Ripley and told her about the incident with the television show. Ripley told Noreen that she was planning on coming down that week anyway. She was delayed in coming because of the preparation and taping of the television show. Ripley asked her mother to pay the airfare. They arranged that she would sleep at Noreen's during her stay.

* * *

Two weeks had passed, and Camay's conscience was working overtime. She had visited Roseway a few times, but noticed no improvement. A couple of times, Joseph dropped by her house for coffee and just to vent a little of the frustration he was feeling at not seeing any improvement. He didn't know what else to do. Each time, Camay felt terrible for not saying anything. She was convinced that she should keep her word to Roseway. Now two weeks had gone by. Joseph stopped over for one of his visits. Camay had the coffee ready and some freshly baked cookies. This time, Camay wanted to pray before they indulged. Joseph was fine with that.

"Heavenly Father, we thank you for this day and for the blessings you lavish on us. Forgive us, Lord, for the times we often take those blessings for granted. We ask that you would bless our time together and our conversation. Amen."

Joseph was surprised by the prayer. "Thank you for praying, Camay. That was a little out of the ordinary for us."

"Yes, well, I feel I need to discuss something very important with you. It has been eating away at me for a couple of weeks. I could sure use God's help right now. I have been putting it off because I didn't think it was my place to tell you. However, my conscience is telling me otherwise.

"Something did happen that night at your house. I feel terrible about it, and somewhat responsible, because it involves my son Samson. I'll just be blunt and truthful. That night, I went down to your house to borrow something from Roseway. When I got there, I was shocked to find Samson and Roseway together in the kitchen in what I would call a very compromising position. Samson explained everything to me when I took him home. That night, when I walked into your house, I was so surprised. I made Roseway feel very guilty and ashamed of what they had done. I really came down hard on her. I told her she better tell you what happened. I gave her two weeks or I would tell you. Samson told me that when he drove her home the night of the dinner, they were drawn to each other, and one thing lead to another, and they had intercourse in the car. The next day Samson went to see her again. When he arrived, there she was dressed in her bathrobe. That is when I caught them together. When I left Rose that night, she was no doubt very upset. I'm so sorry, Joseph."

Joseph just sat there like his heart was being ripped from his chest. He couldn't believe it. Never in a million years would he ever have imagined Roseway would do that to him. Joseph didn't say a word. He just stood up from the table and walked out of the house. Camay yelled at him to encourage him to stay and talk, but he was so determined he just rushed out of the house. He got in his car and spun out of the driveway like a crazy man. He was swerving the car from one side of the road to the other, screaming at the top of his lungs. The car hit a rut in the road and the right front tire blew, spinning the car to a stop. The back end of the car half hung over the mountain road embankment.

He just cried and cried with a lion-like roar. "Oh God, you were right. I don't believe it. Why would she do that to us?" He pounded on the steering wheel with his fist. Tears stuck to the corners of his eyes. "We waited so long for each other. What we had was special. We were so pure before each other. Now she defiled her body with some guy she barely even knew. It makes me feel sick. Oh God, didn't she love me? She couldn't have been in her right mind. That was the one thing Rose was always so adamant about. Things always had to be done in a Godly way. What on earth happened? Why God? Why?"

MY SON JOSEPH, THE AMAZING THING IS STILL YET TO COME; THE TIME OF RECKONING, WHEN YOU WILL NOT ONLY BELIEVE WHAT HAPPENED, BUT ACCEPT THE TRUTH. WITH MY UNDERSTANDING, YOU WILL BE ABLE TO FORGIVE ROSEWAY AND LOVE HER EVEN MORE

"Forgive her, how will I ever be able to forgive her? I'm so angry right now that I just want to go shake her until she tells me that this is not true. Is that why she tried to kill herself? My God, did I push her into another man's arms? Was I really that mean to her? What do I do now? I don't want to see her. I'm afraid of what

I might do. I have to think this through, try and make some kind of sense of all that has happened. Oh, God, I need your help."

20
Face to Face

Ripley's plane landed. Noreen settled her in at the house and informed her of all the details. Ripley wanted to know everything so she would be better prepared for visiting Roseway.

Joseph came to the house to talk to Noreen. He was not aware that Ripley was there. When he entered through the doorway, he was a little surprised. "Ripley, you are back again."

"Yes, I am. Just like a bad penny," she commented, reading the coldness within his dark eyes.

"Well, I wouldn't say that. It is actually good you are here. You were right. Rose and I got married too soon. She wasn't ready. I guess I wasn't, either." The tone in his voice was sinister. His eyes were dark. Anger covered his face like an evil mask. He was hurt and sad. He gripped the back of the chair as if to hold himself upright and strong. If he let go of the chair he might just fall to his knees and weep in a puddle of despair.

Noreen piped up defensively. "What are you talking about, Joseph?"

Joseph's tone was a little agitated. "Noreen, you don't know the half of it." His breathing was heavy as his heart was still pumping as if he had just finished a marathon.

Noreen could see that he was acting strangely. "What don't I know? What on earth happened?"

With a deep sigh, Joseph began. "Well, last night I had a talk with Camay."

"Who?" Ripley asked.

Joseph responded to her like she was an uninformed idiot. "Camay! She is our neighbour. She lives about a mile from our house. Anyway, Camay told me everything I didn't want to hear. Noreen, your daughter had an affair on me when I was away."

Shocked, Noreen looked at him like he was from another planet and she hadn't heard correctly. "What did you say? Did you say what I think you said? That can't be true."

"I assure you that it is true. Camay wouldn't tell me a story like that and incriminate her own son, Samson."

There was silence in the room. Joseph blurted out, "I would just like to get my hands around Samson's neck and break it like a twig."

Ripley was concerned with Joseph's angry bursts, but at the same time she could sympathize with him. She wheeled her chair over to him. "Are you okay? Is there anything I can do to help?"

"I'm fine, just hurt and angry at her. It's weird. I just came from seeing her at the hospital. When I went there I was so angry, I just wanted to shake her and snap her out of it, so I could give her hell. When I looked at her, my heart sank. I'm still angry at the situation and hurt by what she did. The fact is I love her."

Ripley thought for a moment. "It does paint a different picture. Knowing Rose the way I do, I imagine she felt as distressed about what she did as you feel. That is not in keeping with her normal behaviour or her moral beliefs. There had to be something more going on with her, probably a compilation of events."

Joseph interjected. "What difference does it make? She did it."

Noreen was saddened by the news. She felt for Joseph. He must feel so betrayed by it. What could she say? Roseway was her daughter. She felt bad for both of them. All she could do was try to appease his pain with an apology. "I'm sorry that you have to go through this. What are you going to do?"

"I don't know right now. I'll stay at the farm. I have to work to pay the bills. Please, give me some time to think and pray. I'm not going to make any rash decisions. Let's just get Roseway well again."

"I've got to go," Joseph said, curling up his lip and wiping the water from his eyes.

Ripley asked, "Could you drop me off at the hospital on your way home?"

"Sure."

Joseph lifted Ripley into his truck and put her wheelchair in the back of the truck. Ripley looked off into the field as the trees moved passed the window. Joseph clenched his teeth. He wanted to talk more, but didn't know exactly what he wanted to say. Part of him blamed Ripley. *If it wasn't for her, we would have gone on that honeymoon. Things would have been great.* That was his easy way out.

Ripley felt distant from Joseph, even though she sat beside him. *I wonder if this is how Roseway felt when she sat in this truck with him a few weeks back. Two people can be so close, yet so far away.* She also sensed his pain. She wanted to say something that didn't sound stupid or insensitive. "Joseph, did you know I almost didn't make it back? In fact, I was clinically dead for a short time. The experience really gave me an entirely new perspective on life. Things are not always the way they seem to be when we go through these times of trial. There is always more than meets the eye. God sees it all, but often we don't. Sometimes we are so busy looking at the problem that we don't recognise the solutions."

"Yes, I am well aware of the problem. I'm trying hard to find the answers."

"What if God gave you all the answers? Would that change the way you feel?"

"That is a good question. I would like to think that it would change the way I feel in some small way."

"Even if the answers showed you that you were to blame for what happened?"

"What, are you saying that I am to blame?"

"No, I'm not saying that at all. You are misunderstanding me. Isn't it human nature to always have to blame someone if something goes wrong? I learned that it is better to correct the wrongs in our lives rather than spend our lives looking for someone to blame, for the whys of this world. It is better to trust that God will work it all out for good. We don't see it when we go through it. Nor do we understand it. God does know all things and He understands. If we seek his understanding, someday it will all make sense. Until then we put one foot in front of the other and move forward together. What are you going to do?"

"Honestly Ripley, I don't know right now. I think I need to get away and pray and think about how I really feel. How will I ever trust her again? When someone destroys that trust, it is hard to get it back." His eyes filled with tears.

Ripley's heart felt his hurt. He drove the truck to the hospital's front entrance, pulled out her wheelchair, then lifted Ripley in his strong arms. She hugged him tightly and kissed him on the cheek, then whispered, "Joseph, I know that God can heal your heart and he can heal your marriage. The two of you are not in this alone. We have a great God who wants you both to have a wonderful marriage, the way it is meant to be."

He placed her in the chair. "Thanks, Ripley, for what you said. Take care of Roseway for me, will ya? You seem to do a better job of it than I."

"Joseph, I have always sensed a jealousy from you in regards to the friendship Rose and I share. Jealousy can be such a killer. Lord knows I've been jealous of the two of you. I realized how foolish I was to be jealous. For Rose's sake, I put those feelings away. Please, Joseph, try to do the same. Rose didn't choose me over you when I was in that coma. She followed her heart. I don't want it to be a competition between you and me. I would back away from her friendship in a second if I thought that I was breaking the two of you apart. I don't want that hanging over me. I hope that I can be your friend as much as I am Rose's friend. Think about it. I know that has been a major problem for you. I'm sorry you didn't have the Hawaii honeymoon. You have each other for a lifetime. What will you do?"

"I'm going to take off for a couple of weeks. We will see ..." Joseph jumped back in his truck and drove away.

When Ripley arrived at Roseway's room, there was a nurse trying to feed her.

"Come on now, Roseway, you have to eat your food to keep up your strength."

Roseway spit her food on the floor. Ripley sat back and watched in disbelief, remembering the first time she met Roseway. She had been so feisty and determined. Ripley thought of all the times that Roseway took care of her. It wasn't that long ago that Roseway was feeding Ripley. Now it was her turn to help Roseway, and she was determined to succeed. *God, you said I would be helping women. Little did I know, one of those women would be Roseway. Lord, please help me to help her.* Ripley wheeled her chair over to Roseway, and took the spoon from the nurse. “Please let me try and feed her.”

Ripley looked at Roseway. “Hello Pal, It’s me, Rip. The nurse is right. You need to eat your food. Look, I’m eating it.” She took a spoonful of food and almost gagged, but pretended it tasted good. “Here, now it is your turn.” Ripley put the food up to Roseway’s mouth. Her mouth opened like a baby being fed. She was chewing the food, and then spit it right into Ripley’s face. Ripley scratched her head in disbelief, grabbed the towel from the table and wiped away the food. She tried to remain tolerant. After all, Roseway didn’t know what she was doing.

Ripley made an excuse. “I don’t blame you. That food tastes terrible.”

Ripley poured some water onto the towel to wipe Roseway’s face. When she was wiping her face, Roseway bit Ripley’s hand.

“Ouch!” she screamed. “Hey, that hurt.” Realizing that she had feeling in her hand again diminished the shock of what Roseway did. It didn’t stop Ripley from taking Roseway’s hand and biting her back. Roseway pulled her hand away and looked at the bite marks. Then she slapped Ripley across the face. Ripley promptly responded by hitting Roseway across her face. Ripley realized that Roseway was being stimulated and responding. She knew that up until this point in time, there was no response except on the night she saw Hattley Street.

Ripley pushed a little further. “Rose, you are being a little brat today. What are you so angry about? Are you angry because Big Joe hurt you all the time? Are you angry at me for being the reason you never had a honeymoon? Are you angry at your mother because when you were a little girl, she never came to rescue you from BJ? Maybe you are angry at Joseph for leaving you at the farm.”

Mumbled sounds came from Roseway's mouth. The statements Ripley was saying were starting to upset her. "What is it, Rose? What are you trying to say? Tell me, Rose. Come on, honey, speak to me. Are you angry at God? Do you feel he let you down? Rose, I think you are angry for all those reasons. More than that I think you are angry at yourself because you made a terrible mistake. You are human, Rose. That is right, Rose, we know about you and Samson. That is why you tried to kill yourself and make all that anger and pain go away. Isn't that right, Rose? Tell me." Ripley raised her voice. "Say it, Rose. You can admit it, Rose. Admit it."

Roseway started to cry.

With a loud, bottomless roar came a piercing, "YES. Yes, I'm angry!"

Ripley reached out to Roseway, reading the fear in Roseway's eyes. "Everything is going to be alright."

Rose looked around feeling somewhat strange, not fully aware of where she was at that moment. Feeling somewhat confused, she spoke quietly. "Is Joseph home yet?"

Ripley spoke cautiously as not to upset Rose. "Everything is fine, Rose. You are in the hospital. Do you realize where you are?"

She looked around the room. It was more than familiar. "Yes, I think I'm in the hospital."

"Rose, do you remember what happened?"

Roseway looked off to the side, like she was pushing a rewind button on a video. "Yesterday, I was in the bathtub. Then I fell asleep. Now, I just woke up here in the hospital. Why am I in the hospital?"

"Rose, you have been in the hospital for more than three weeks. I know you don't remember, and that is okay. You hurt yourself in the bathtub. Joseph found you. He called an ambulance and they brought you here to make you better. Do you remember anything about the last few weeks?"

She stuttered, "N-no, I don't remember. Where is Joseph now? When is he coming to see me?"

"He had to go away on a trip. I'm not sure when he will be back. Do you remember having dinner at Camay's house?"

"Yes, I had fun. I met her kids: Nathan, Nicole and Samson." Rose's eyes started to blink nervously as a memory flashed into her mind. She wanted to ignore it. Samson's face kept flashing into her thoughts. He kissed her ... the memory played out ... "Oh, Ripley, I remember something." Rose closed her eyes with shame. She didn't even want to look her friend in the eye.

Her head went down. Ripley lifted Rose's head in her hands. "It's okay, Rose. It's okay. God will help you work everything out. He knows about you and Samson. Joseph loves you and I know you love him. You will work through this together. Just give him some time. Okay?"

"Does Joseph know about Samson and me?

"Yes Rose, he does know."

"How could Joseph ever forgive me for committing adultery? He deserves better. I'm just evil like my father."

"Stop it, Rose. Those thoughts are all lies from Satan. Don't believe a one of them. You are a child of God."

Roseway wanted to explain her thoughts. "There is this girl who keeps visiting me. She keeps saying bad things to me. Her name is Doubt. She said that she is a part of me. I see her sometimes, but nobody else sees her. Am I crazy?"

"No Rose, you are not crazy. I tell you what, Rose, we will pray and ask God to make her go away. If she tries to come back again and starts telling you bad things, just pray and she should go away. If she doesn't go away, just remember that she is a little girl and she doesn't know anything but lies. She is not a real person, even though she may look real. When you see her, pray and then ignore her. Okay, Rose? You can call me any time or call your mom and we can pray with you, too. If ever you get that feeling of being overwhelmed again, promise me you will call someone? "

"Oh Ripley, I promise. I literally screwed up though, didn't I? I was too ashamed to ask anyone to help me."

"It was a mistake. It is nothing that can't be fixed with time." Ripley wanted to ease up the conversation by changing the subject with a little of her humour. "Rose, remind me never to get in fight with you. I think I have a permanent handprint on my face." Ripley laughed, rubbing her cheek with her hand.

With half of a grin, Roseway said, "I'm sorry."

Dr. Ross kept Roseway in the hospital under supervision for a couple of weeks. In that time, they counselled her regularly so they could make an accurate assessment. In psychological terms, they determined that Rose was experiencing schizophrenia. They were going to control her condition with medication.

It became more complicated when the blood tests revealed that Roseway was also pregnant. When Ripley heard this news, she decided to stay on a little longer. She was very worried about Roseway's mental condition. The entire situation seemed to be such a mess. Ripley had her degree in counselling, and was happy to use what she had learned to help Roseway and Joseph. It also interested her to work with other patients.

The hospital was impressed with Ripley's credentials and the progress Roseway made while working with Ripley. They offered her a job counselling patients in the psychiatric ward. That brought a difficult decision for Ripley to make. Would she stay in Kelowna, accept the job, continue to help Roseway and re-root her life? Or should she stay in Prince George and help her friend Abby with the music business and work in ministry with her? She wanted to do both. How could she be in two places at once? This was not a decision she felt she could make right away. She sought God for His guidance and took time to hear His answer.

21
A Little Surprise

Joseph was away visiting his parents in Coquitlam when Doctor Ross discovered Roseway was pregnant. Doctor Ross sat down with Roseway and gently told her about the pregnancy. "Hello, Roseway, you look much better this week. How are you feeling?"

"Okay, I guess. It would be nice if I could get out of here."

"Well, it won't be too much longer. Have you been feeling depressed?"

"A little, that is because Joseph has not come to visit for a couple weeks. I know he needs some time. He is probably really hurt and mad at me. I don't blame him. It does make me feel sad."

"Have you had anymore thoughts about hurting yourself?"

"No. My friend Ripley and my mom have been helping me a lot."

"Well Rose, your blood test came back and we discovered something disturbing."

Roseway was wondering what could be more disturbing than what has already happened. Doctor Ross didn't make much small talk before he straight out told her, "You are pregnant."

Roseway's eyes widened. "I am? Oh no!" Sarcastically, she thought, *this is just great. Why not make it twins.*

"Why did you say that?" Doctor Ross asked.

With an agitated tone of voice, she snapped, "Because it just complicates things even more. What am I supposed to do? I don't even know if Joseph loves me anymore. Maybe he is going to divorce me. How can I raise a child on my own?"

Dr. Ross tried to give her sound options. "Rose, I can certainly understand your many concerns. There is also a concern that the baby may be born with some defects because of the drugs we gave to you when you first came to the hospital. We didn't know that you were pregnant at that time. It is still very early in your pregnancy. We will find out more when the foetus is a little bigger and we do more tests."

"Do we know who the father is?" Roseway asked. Her thoughts were spinning with questions. *How did I get myself into this mess? How on earth am I going to tell Joseph this along with everything else that has gone on?*

"I'm sorry, we don't know that information. We would have to get a blood sample from the men that you had intercourse with. There were two different men, is that correct?"

Still feeling ashamed to answer the question, her eyes looked down to the floor. "Yes, that is right."

"There is always another option for you to consider and that is medical termination or abortion. During the first forty-nine days of pregnancy, a medical termination is possible without surgery. Medical abortion uses two different drugs, methotrexate or mifepristone, which may be followed by another drug called misoprostol. While these drugs cause an abortion without surgical procedures such as dilation and vacuum, they do take longer to work than surgical abortion. Medical abortion involves several appointments and it often results in a fair amount of cramping and bleeding at home. If a medical abortion isn't successful, you'll need a surgical abortion if you want an abortion.You wouldn't have too many concerns. You are early in your pregnancy. It is a very simple procedure. If you wait past the forty-nine days, then it becomes more complicated. We would put you into a light sleep. When you awaken, it will be gone."

"Either way, wouldn't that be killing the baby?" She didn't know much about abortion. The thought of removing a baby seemed wrong. Then again, she had never been in this situation before.

Convincingly, Doctor Ross continued, "Technically, we don't call it a baby until it actually develops in the mother's womb. The size it is at this time is probably not even an inch long. It is more like a blob. In medical terms, it is called a foetus. Anyway, Rose, take some time to consider what it is that you want to do, okay? I'll come by to see you again in a day or two."

"Okay, Doctor Ross. Thanks for telling me." *Are you sure a grenade didn't fall out of your doctor bag? It is almost like you enjoyed telling me that news.* She faked a smile and waved as he walked out of the room.

Roseway just sat numbed by it all. She wanted Joseph to come by and see her so much. Even if he came by and yelled at her, it would be better than sitting, waiting and wondering what he thinks, what he is planning to do.

After speaking with Roseway, Doctor Ross talked to Noreen and Ripley about the pregnancy and tried to convince them that it might be wiser for Roseway to have a medical termination. He also told them that he already explained the concerns to Roseway. He didn't feel that emotionally she could make a decision of that magnitude at this time. He was not convinced Roseway was capable of handling a nine-month pregnancy, let alone caring for a baby. Doctor Ross also told them he was concerned about the effects some of the medications Roseway was given may have had on the development of the foetus.

Both Ripley and Noreen hit the roof. There was no way they would agree to that. The doctor said that technically speaking, they could leave the decision up to Roseway, being that she is the one carrying the foetus in her womb.

Ripley protested indomitably. "Doctor, an abortion would be the worst thing that Rose could do. I don't think you realize the emotional side effects women go through after having an abortion. They can be devastating. If need be, Noreen or myself would help Rose raise this baby."

Noreen added, "That is right, Doctor. Don't let us forget that there is one other person involved in the life of this baby, and that is the father, whether it is Joseph or Samson. God, I hope it is Joseph's baby. I'll try and get a hold of Joseph. I know he is out of town right now. As soon as he gets back, he will be in here with his blood test. I'll make sure of that. He has had enough time to think about what he wants to do. He either loves my daughter or he doesn't."

Ripley interjected, "Calm down, Noreen. Let's just deal with this situation rationally. Don't panic. Doctor Ross, I'm going to talk to Rose. If you will allow us some time to iron out some of these concerns, one at time, I'm sure a decision will be made that will be best for everyone involved."

Doctor Ross replied, "Not a problem. I'll be back in to see Rose in two days to see how she is doing."

22
Love Hopes

Camay heard Joseph's rig drive past her house. Noreen had spoken to Camay and asked her to get Joseph to call her as soon as he arrived back home. Camay got in her car and hurried over to the farm. Joseph was just getting down from the rig when she pulled in the driveway.

Anxiously, Camay waved at Joseph to get his attention. "Hey Joseph, Noreen wants you to call her as soon as possible. She said it is urgent."

"What is wrong? Is Rose alright? She didn't ...?"

"I don't know. She just told me to get you to call her as soon as you get back."

"Okay, thanks."

Joseph ran into the house and called Noreen. Noreen answered on the first ring. Looking at the number on call display, she said, "Hello, Joseph? I'm glad you are back. Can you come over to my house right away? I need to talk to you about something important. I don't want to tell you over the phone."

"Sure, I'm just going to change and I'll be right there."

Joseph quickly tore off his soiled clothing and jumped into the shower. He had been thinking all week about his marriage to Rose. He also stopped over and stayed a night with his parents in

Coquitlam. They had a long talk. His parents always raised Joseph to be a good Christian man. He knew every bible story ever told. As a Christian, he had always understood the concept of forgiveness. Never before was he put in a position that would test that belief. After a week of prayer and meditation, he was sure he could forgive Rose for what happened. The trusting would take a while to restore. He loved her and he had no doubt about it. He dressed himself in a collared blue shirt, and put on some cologne because he planned to go and see Roseway right after his visit with Noreen.

He knocked on the old wooden door. Noreen invited him in. "Have a seat."

"Ms. Shaffer, what is it you want to talk to me about?"

"First of all, I would like to know if you ever plan on getting back together with Roseway."

"Ms. Shaffer, I never left her. I just needed some time. I wasn't ready to face her right away. I know she snapped out of it, but I didn't know what to say to her because I didn't know how I felt. There was never a doubt that I love her; my question is, how much does she love me to do what she did? I can forgive her because I love her. When we said our vows, I meant every word. I married her for better or worse."

Noreen was relieved to hear Joseph's perspective. "I know that Rose loves you, too. She needs you more than you know. Emotionally, she is doing pretty well, considering what she has been through. Physically, there is a complication." Noreen paused.

"What?"

"Joseph, Rose is pregnant."

Sitting there processing what Noreen just said, he sighed and looked stone-faced. "You have got to be kidding me. What will be next? Under any other circumstance, I would be thrilled. The timing couldn't be any worse."

Noreen blurted, "Perhaps this is God's timing. His timing is perfect."

"I would be happier if I knew that she was carrying my child. Is it my baby?"

"We don't know, son. You could take a blood test to find out."

He bit his fingernail while he thought, and his knee bounced up and down nervously. "I would like to know for myself. Maybe it would be better if I didn't know? That way, I could just raise the child like it was my own. I hope the baby is mine, otherwise every time I look at that child I will be reminded of what Rose did. If the child is Samson's, just maybe Roseway would rather divorce me and marry him? What do you think?"

"Oh, Joseph, I think you and Roseway need to talk and work these things out together."

Trying to process his thoughts, Joseph scratched his head and agreed. "You are right. I should go over and see her. I put it off long enough. How is she coping with this news?"

Noreen pursed her lips then nodded her head. "She seems to be holding together. It would do her a world of good to see you."

"I'm going over there now." He felt a need to impress her. "How do I look?"

Noreen smiled. "You look like a handsome, loving husband who will someday become a wonderful father."

Noreen phoned Roseway at the hospital to tell her Joseph was on the way over. Roseway felt like a school girl getting ready for her first date. She changed her clothing, put on a white angora sweater that accentuated a pleasing glow to her face. Her hair was shiny and clean, brushed down over her shoulders. Attempting to make everything look perfect, she fidgeted with the things on her side table. She put on a little lipstick, then wiped it off. It made her feel cheap. The butterflies in her stomach felt more like giant seagulls tossing over the ocean waves. Time seemed to slow as she waited with trepidation, wondering what Joseph would say.

Joseph poked his head around the corner of the door. "Anybody home?" *She looks stunning, as always.*

Roseway's face lit up like a lantern. He walked over to her bed and sat down beside her. He handed her a beautiful red rose.

She thanked him with a kiss on the cheek. *He smells so good. I've missed him so much.*

"You look great, Rose. A lot better than you looked the last time I saw you. I hear you are feeling much better now." *Protect your heart. Keep a bit of a distance.*

Roseway felt an awkwardness she had never before felt with Joseph. Perhaps it was the guilt she herself was feeling. *I wonder if he is picturing Samson and me together when he looks at me. I've got to break passed this.*

Seeing the sadness in his eyes, she wanted to reach out to him and hold him like she had before all this happened. It felt like forever since she felt his loving embrace. Only words stuttered from her lips. "I'm so sorry, Joseph. I really messed up. There is no excuse for what I did. I know that. I don't know what to say to you."

He wanted to console her, seeing the sincere remorse written all over her face. It was difficult to let his hurt fall away. If only it had never happened, but it did. That was the problem he had to resolve within his own heart. "Rose, I'm well aware of what you did. That is all I've thought about for the last couple of weeks. What you did, hurt me to the depth of my soul. It was a betrayal I never would have expected from you. However, it happened. While we can't take it back or pretend it never happened, we can and must move on together and work through our feelings. The one thing I know to be true is that I love you, Rose. My question is, do you love me? Do you?"

Roseway couldn't hold herself back any longer. She lunged at him, wrapping her arms around Joseph and just cried and sobbed in his arms. "Yes, I love you, Joseph. I've loved you since the first day we met."

Joseph soaked in her hug. For a brief moment, he felt the urge to pull away from her and punish her for the way she had made him feel. Then he realized the solution. It was his pulling away from her that pushed her into Samson's arms. He felt her sobs soaking his shirt. If ever anyone cried with such regret, it was Roseway. An unbelievable feeling of empathy flowed from the deepest part of his spirit—compassion, and a redeeming love. Joseph held her tight and wiped the tears away from her cheeks. While she was crying, Rose pulled her head back and looked Joseph in the face. "There is one more thing you need to know."

He cupped her head in his hands and kissed her lips and then whispered, "I know. We are going to become parents." *I can't believe it.*

Rose's crying began to subdue, and she hugged him like she never wanted to let him go again. *Should I mention the blood test? That must be a difficult thing to accept.* "Honey, do you want to have a blood test to find out if you are the father?"

"I'm not going to lie to you. It would mean a lot to me to know if the child is of my gene pool. It does bother me to think that it is possible you are carrying Samson's child. For now, we can wait until you are a little farther along in your pregnancy. We don't need to know this right now. I'm not going anywhere. Do you want to work on our marriage, have this baby, and raise him or her together? Is Samson permanently out of our lives?"

"Oh yes, Joseph. He is gone and I promise you, nothing like that will ever happen again." Roseway thanked him for being so understanding. They continued to hug each other.

Ripley wheeled her chair into the room, not noticing Joseph at first. Then she began to back up. "Oh, sorry, I didn't mean to interrupt the two of you. I'll come back later."

Joseph stopped her. "It is okay, come on in."

"Are you sure? The two of you look like you are having much needed time together."

23
The Weaving Road

Over the next couple of months, many changes took place. Ripley moved in at the farm with Roseway and Joseph. Ripley decided to take the job at the hospital, working part-time until she felt assured that Roseway didn't need her help any longer. The pregnancy was developing nicely, except for the morning sickness. Joseph kept working. He was somewhat comforted knowing Roseway was not alone at the farm all the time. There was still a little bit of a trust issue that Joseph needed to overcome. That would take time.

Ripley was enjoying Roseway's pregnancy more than Roseway was enjoying it. They had a lot of fun looking at baby books, looking for baby names, picking out colours for the baby's room. Noreen had a baby shower and invited all the people who were at their wedding. Even Joseph was getting a little excited about the thought of becoming a father. He never did have the blood test to find out if the baby was his or Samson's. Joseph and Roseway convinced themselves that the baby was indeed Joseph's. That was good enough for him.

The months went by and the baby's movements became stronger. Ripley was often reminded of her own pregnancy that ended way too soon. The abortion still bothered her a little. She knew she was forgiven, but watching Roseway going through the different stages often made her wish she could have experienced it for herself. Now that she was paralysed, she didn't think it was likely she would ever get married or have a baby of her own. Perhaps God had a different calling for her life. She believed it to be true and was motivated by that faith. Through Rose's pregnancy, she would enjoy the experience as much as she could.

They had become such good friends since that day they met four years ago at that dumpster. It almost seemed like it was yesterday. The wheels of change were always turning. There was an undeniable bond of friendship between them. At times, it made Joseph a little jealous. Joseph loved Roseway so much that her happiness meant more to him than his insecurities. He would shake off those feelings whenever they crept into his mind. Deep down, he knew in his heart that Ripley only wanted what was best for Roseway. She was a great friend to both of them.

Ripley's progress seemed to move slowly. There was little change in the paralysis in her legs, although her arms had regained feeling. Abby and Ripley called each other every week. One day while Ripley was on the phone, Roseway eavesdropped on their conversation.

"Hello Abby, how are things going? Have you written any more songs this week?"

"Actually, yes, I have. You have to hear this latest song. I think it is the best yet. We have to record them sometime soon. We were asked to be the special music at a ladies' fellowship meeting at the Lake Ridge Baptist Church. When are you coming home?"

"Oh, that is so exciting. I can't wait to hear the new song. You will have to play it for me in a couple of weeks. I have to come back to Prince George and get more of my things, and I also have to go for my annual blood tests. I kind of put having the tests on the back-burner with all that has gone on. I've been getting headaches again."

"That doesn't sound good. I'm glad you are going back for a check-up."

"I'm pretty sure that I am going to stay in Kelowna permanently. I really like working with the patients at the hospital. I'll have to get my own place soon. When Rose has the baby, then I'll move into my own place. I can't live here forever. Moving here was a hard decision to make, because I really feel like we should be doing our ministry together. I don't see how I can do both, unless you move here, too. I was thinking that maybe you could consider the idea? Besides, I miss you."

"I really miss you, too, Ripley. Going to therapy by myself is not as much fun. To answer your question, yes, I have been seriously considering a change. I was thinking of putting the brownstone up for sale. If it sells, then maybe we could get a place together in Kelowna near the hospital. That way we can help each other with the financial matters and we still do ministry together. It would take me a little time to re-establish a clientele of music students."

Ripley was very excited at the idea. "That is so exciting. Anyway, I'll be back in Prince George in a couple of weeks."

"Are you sure your friend will be okay on her own? What if she loses it again?"

"Rose is doing fine. At some point she is going to have to stand on her own two feet again. I know she can take care of herself. Maybe I'm holding her back staying here. It would be good for her to regain that independence she used to have. She is tougher than many people think. Anyway, I'll be home in a couple of weeks. Not sure for how long. I'll have to come back here to be with Rose until the baby is born. That will be so awesome if you move here. You and Roseway can meet each other. It will be great. Oh, I'm so excited. Life is grand. Anyway, I better go. I'll talk to you in a couple of weeks when I come down for the tests."

Roseway walked into the room as Ripley put down the phone receiver. "I couldn't help but hear you on the phone. Was that your friend Abby?" *Why does she have to have her friend Abby come live in Kelowna?*

"Yes, it was. I'd like to get the two of you together some time. I think you two could be great friends."

With a little jealousy in her voice, Rose replied, "I don't need another friend, I have you. You are my best friend."

"Rose, I can appreciate that you feel that way about our friendship. You and I are the best of friends. However, it is not good to put all your eggs in one basket, so to speak. Abby and I share a very special friendship and you and I also share a very special friendship. I think that is good. I wouldn't want to lose either one of your friendships. I love you both. Our friendships with one another are unique on their own. I believe it would be good for you to have other friends besides just me. I can't always be here for you, even if I would like to be. For example, you have helped me many times above and beyond expectation. I appreciate you so much. Rose, you know that you hold a special place in my heart.

"Sometimes our lives just get in the way. When I went back to Kelowna for rehabilitation, you couldn't be there for me, and that was okay. I knew you had a life and responsibilities of your own. During that time, God brought Abby back into my life. It was at a time when I really needed a friend. Abby has also helped me out many times when I was in very needy situations. I will always appreciate her friendship, too. Can you understand what I am trying to say?"

"Yes, when you explain it that way."

"I have to go back to Kelowna and get some more of my things in a couple of weeks. Rose, I think that after you have the baby, I should move out and get my own place. I'll be working full-time by then. It would be easier transporting to work if I live near the hospital. It looks like Abby may move to Kelowna when she sells her place. We might get a place together to save on living expenses."

Roseway didn't like what she was hearing from Ripley. Her heart sank down to her stomach. "Why can't you just stay here? I could get my driving licence and drive you to work every day instead of you taking a cab."

"Please don't get upset about this. Roseway, please understand, I can't stay living here. You and Joseph need to build your family together. Joseph doesn't need me hanging around all the time. Think about him and your baby. He loves you so much. You both need to nurture that love you have for one another. You are going to have a precious little baby soon, who will need all the love and care you can give. It will be better for both you and Joseph to rely on each other. In reality, I think I am just hindering you from doing that in the way you are capable. As long as I am hanging around, I don't think that will happen. You rely on me too much."

Roseway conceded her feelings. "I know you are right, but I'll miss you so much."

"Well, I won't be that far away, just a phone call. We will visit often. Anyway, that is not until the baby is born. So don't worry about it anymore."

The phone rang, interrupting their conversation. It was Ms. Wilks. She phoned to tell Ripley that she received a call from the hospital informing her that Ripley's father, Amadeus, had passed away that morning. He left a Will of Testament with the nurse at the hospital. His only request was for Ripley to use the money from his estate to set up a Rape Crisis Centre that would be helpful to both men and women who have a rape crisis. He didn't want any funeral. With his last dying breath, he whispered his last words to the nurse who was holding his hand: "Tell Ripley I'll be okay." Ripley hung up the phone. She told Roseway about the visit she had with her father a little while back.

"The last time I saw my father, we knew we wouldn't see each other again. I was a little sad when I said goodbye to him that day. Now, for some strange reason, I'm not sad to hear that he has passed away. I know that he had salvation. My heart feels comforted to know I forgave him for what he did to me. What he did to me was horrible, but God helped me to forgive him. In the realm of eternity, what he did seems so insignificant in comparison to what he may be doing right now, or where he is at this very moment. Can we even begin to imagine for one moment what it would be like to walk into the arms of a Saviour, to walk from death into life? It is all in one's perspective."

Rose agreed. "That is for sure. Who can ever really understand the eternal when we live in the temporal? Not me."

24
The Dance

The brownstone was decorated with balloons and streamers. Abby hobbled to the door without her crutches, and opened the door with her arms wide open. "Welcome home, Ripley. It feels so good to have you home again. It seems like you have been gone forever."

They gave each other a long hug. Abby helped Ripley with her bag and asked, "How was the bus ride?"

"Not too bad at all. We made pretty good time. It has been a while since I've seen you. I think we have a lot of catching up to do. Any bites with the sale of the house?"

Abby tried to hide the truth to surprise Ripley. "Well, not a one." Her smile could not conceal the truth. "No bites on the house, but I do have a buyer! I'll be moving to Kelowna in ninety days, if the deal goes through."

If Ripley could have jumped up and down, she would have. Instead she danced in her chair. "That is great news! Perfect timing, too."

Abby and Ripley made the most of their two-week visit. They stayed up late at night and watched old movies. They spent many days working on new songs. Abby was insistent that they record a few songs. They spent some time in the recording studio. The ladies' fellowship at the Baptist church was a great evening. Many of the ladies left that evening feeling so touched by the music and the words they ministered to them. Five more ladies accepted Christ at that fellowship.

It was the day before Ripley was to return to Kelowna that she had to go to find out the results of the tests that she had taken the week earlier. Abby drove Ripley to the doctor's appointment. Ripley insisted that Abby go in with her to see the doctor. Ripley always dreaded the visits, never knowing what to expect. It was the waiting that ate away at her.

Doctor Spandecker sat behind his grey desk, looking at Ripley's information and test results on his high-tech computer screen. His face looked very solemn. He began to tell Ripley the reason for the reoccurring headaches. "Ripley, the scan showed a very disturbing discovery. When Doctor Brown operated on you to remove the tumours, he could only remove the one tumour because of the complications they had on the operating table. They didn't want to continue any longer for fear of losing you again. That remaining tumour is a malignant Glioblastomas. Sometimes this kind of tumour can be removed. In your case, it has already spread rapidly into the surrounding brain tissue attached to the temporal lobe. It has not responded well to the treatment or medication that you have been taking. The tumour has in fact grown. By looking at the scan, surgery is not an option. That is why you have not regained the feeling in your legs.

Ripley looked at Doctor Spandecker like he was just reading someone else's chart. She looked over to Abby, whose face looked like she just lost her best friend. All Ripley could say was, "Wow, I'm going to die. I don't believe it."

Abby freaked out. "What do you mean there is nothing you can do? There has to be something you can do to help her."

Doctor Spandeker continued. "Glioblastomas can be difficult to treat, although in some cases radiation therapy, steroids, and chemotherapy sometimes prolong survival. What we can try is a much higher dose of chemotherapy. However, for this type of tumour and where it is located, there is only a very small chance that chemo would do any good. Without chemotherapy, you may live six months to a year. With the chemotherapy your life may be extended past a year, but only if it slowed the growth of the tumour.

"However, you would be a very sick young lady. The quality of life during that extra time may not be worth it. Do you want quality of life, or quantity? The decision is up to you. If you want to try the highest dosage of chemotherapy, we can begin this week or you could leave it in God's hands."

"I didn't think I would be dying quite so soon. This doesn't make sense to me. Well, I want quality of life. I would also like to live to be a nice old lady. I am a woman of God, but it would not be my choice to die now or in the near future. Saying that, my life is not my own. I will leave it in God's hands."

Abby questioned her decision. "Ripley, are you sure you don't want to take the chance? Just maybe that small percentage will save you."

Tears welled up in Ripley's eyes and with a heart so sincere and loving she cried, "My dear friend Abby, the doctor said it would only prolong my life for a short time. It has been difficult enough learning to accept the fact that I would be in this wheelchair for the rest of my life. If I can enjoy the next six months to a year living life with the people I love, then I would have lived a lifetime happy. I don't want to spend the rest of my life in a hospital, vomiting and pissing my pants."

The doctor suggested, "I'll prescribe you some steroid medication and painkillers. The intensity of the headaches most likely will increase as the tumour grows and the pressure builds. Hopefully, the steroids will slow the growth of the tumour. You may also experience mood swings, dizziness. I will forward all the information to Doctor West in Kelowna and he can follow up with you regularly. I'll leave you two alone now so you can discuss things. Take all the time you need."

Abby hugged her friend and they cried together. Abby asked Ripley, "What do you want to do?"

"I want to go and stay at Mother's house for a few weeks. I'll have to tell her and Lauren and spend some time with them. In that time, I would also like to go visit a couple of old friends. Could you take me to see them?" Ripley could hardly speak. "Oh, God, I can't tell Roseway until after the baby is born. It will break her heart. It wouldn't do her or the baby any good to know. I can only hope that God will grant me the time I need before I tell her. I will want to spend the rest of my time at the farm with Rose and Joseph. I hope I get to see their little baby being born. If the doctor is accurate in his estimate, I might just live long enough to see the baby being born and also make sure Roseway is okay.

"My precious friend, Abby, I know I can't get through this without your help. May I call on you to go beyond what I should even ask or expect from you? Would you consider coming to stay at the farm when it is almost time for me to go? I'm sure Roseway won't mind. There are plenty of rooms in that house. I don't want to die in the hospital. I would like to be surrounded by my closest friends and family. You will know when that time is near. When that time comes, could you arrange for this to happen for me?"

Abby was still crying. "Ripley, I'll do whatever you want me to do." *Why God? Why would you allow this to happen to someone who makes such a difference in this world? She loves you, Lord, and wants to live for you.*

The world needs more Christians like her. Please, Lord God, create a miracle in Ripley's life.

Ripley's concern was for Abby and Roseway. *I've got to be strong through this. Getting all mushy will only upset Abby more. I'm not going to feel sorry for myself.* "Alright then, let's get ourselves together. I want to spend the rest of my life laughing, not crying. Okay?"

With a deep sigh, Abby rolled her eyes, took a deep breath and replied, "Okay." *For you Ripley, I'll try even though my heart wants to cry a thousand tears.*

Ripley spent the next couple of days with Abby. They recorded a couple more songs. Abby prayed every night for God to heal Ripley's tumour. Abby did all her crying when she thought Ripley was not around. It bothered Ripley to watch her friend pretending to be happy, when it was obvious that Abby was already feeling the tearing of her heart.

Ripley was going to stay at her mother's house and was leaving the next day. Abby arranged a nice dinner out at the local pub called the Cancun. Abby thought it would be something special to take Ripley back to the place where she once did a lot of dancing. Ripley was quite surprised and happy to see her old boss Mr. Timmins and her old roommates Jim and Jenn, who had lived with Ripley at the warehouse a few years back. The biggest surprise was Ripley's previous boyfriend, Professor JD Cleveland, sitting at the table. It was very difficult for JD to give up his pride and gather up the courage to come after jumping ship. Deep down, he still loved Ripley.

Abby had tracked each one of them down and told them the news. She wanted them all to come and give Ripley the time of her life. Abby warned them beforehand to make sure they brought their smiles. They all did just that. From one funny story to the next, they reminisced. It was a difficult time in their lives when the three of them lived on the street. They all agreed that they learned some valuable life lessons.

Jim had his guitar in hand and he played Ripley's favourite songs. Everyone joined in. JD went over to Ripley and asked her to dance. She looked at him with a puzzled expression. *I can't walk. How can I ever dance again?* JD took Ripley's hand in his and he danced around her chair. They danced around the dance floor with her sitting in the wheelchair. He spun the chair around. She laughed from the deep. Then he lifted Ripley to her feet, and with his arms wrapped around her, he held her upright against his body.

"And you thought you couldn't dance. There are many things I could help you do. Ripley I was a fool." He lavished kisses on her as they slow danced to the music while she leaned against him. Feeling his words being choked by emotion, he spoke softly into her ear, "Ripley, I love you. I'm so sorry that I stopped coming to see you. Do you remember that dumpster called denial that you once told me about? I've kind of been living there myself lately. I couldn't face what happened to you. I guess, in a way, I ran away. Abby told me that you are dying. The thought of living without you really hit hard. It was a wake-up call for me. I was awake all last night thinking, remembering all the fun times we had. I realized that I would rather have you and love you just the way you are right now than not have you in my life at all. Will you marry me?"

Ripley paused for a moment while the music continued to play. *He is asking me now? That is impossible. There is not enough time. Oh, God, what do I say?* "John, I don't know what to say. You caught me by surprise. I'm flattered, but John you don't know what you are asking. Why would you want to marry me? I may not be alive six months from now."

"Six months of loving you and caring for you would be better than not loving you at all. I was planning on asking you after

Roseway's wedding. In fact, I bought this ring for you when I was away at seminar. Then you got sick and everything got all messed up. My judgment became clouded. I needed time to think. Everything makes perfect sense to me now. I know I want you in my life as my wife."

Ripley could see the pain in his eyes and she didn't want him to suffer that pain any longer. Because of the untarnished love she felt toward him, she gently whispered, "John David, you can love me and care about me without marrying me, by loving me with your heart. In such a short time I have come to accept many changes in my life. One of the hardest things to accept was realizing that I would never experience what it feels like to have a man physically love me intimately in the same way I would have if I were not paralyzed. However, John, in the time you and I have dated you have loved me more than any other man ever has. For that I am so thankful. I will cherish your love as long as I live.

"Time does not permit a marriage for you and me. I don't have much time. I have to spread the love I have to many people. If my life was different, the answer would be yes. What I give you is the love that is in my heart and soul. Please take my love with you now and forever, and never forget the love we have shared. Remember me the way we were, the laughter we shared, the deep conversations and kissing under the moonlight. That is what I want you to remember about us. I don't know what else to say to you, except to tell you that I love you. I've known that since the first time I was in your class."

JD gave her one last, long kiss. It seemed to last through to the end of the song. He gently picked her up. She kissed him on the cheek and clandestinely wiped the little tear from his face. He put her back in her chair, then wheeled her back to the table. The night came to a close and everyone went their separate ways. They gave long, forever goodbyes to one another as they left the restaurant.

It was just Ripley and Abby left sitting at the table. Abby was a little curious. "So, what were the two of you whispering about when you were dancing? That was quite the kiss he gave you."

"That, Abby, is top secret. I can't tell."

"Oh, come on. You've got to tell me. We have no secrets."

"He ... asked me to marry him. However, the kiss, well, that was our farewell kiss. It was an amazing kiss. Is it getting hot in here?" Wearing a pleased look on her face, she waved a cool breeze over her warm cheeks. "You know, Abby, when I'm gone, you might want to look up JD's phone number. In fact, I'll give you his phone number. You two would make a good couple."

"Okay, little Miss Matchmaker, let's get you home. You have a big day tomorrow."

"Wait a minute, Abby; please let me tell you something."

Abby bent over to let Ripley whisper in her ear. "I just wanted to say thanks for tonight. I had an amazing time." Ripley kissed Abby on the cheek.

Abby responded with a smile. "You are so welcome. That's what friends are for. Now let's get you home. You are getting as mushy as you say your friend Roseway gets. When I meet Roseway, I'm going to tell her what a mush ball you are becoming."

"Oh, you wouldn't dare."

"Oh, wouldn't I?" Abby laughed.

"Roseway can never find out that I get sentimental. I'll never live it down ... On the other hand, maybe I will."

Abby raised her voice. "That is not even funny. Even when you are dying you have a sick sense of humour."

With her typical grin, Ripley recanted. "Sorry."

They both laughed all the way back to the brownstone.

Abby helped Ripley to her bed. Ripley reached for her bible and read a couple of pages. In the quiet of the room, her mixed emotions ran wild like fire consuming a dry bush. The reality was crashing down on her. To see her friends and JD for what may have been the last time really made an impact on her. Ripley had a moment of anger arise within her as she thought of each person in her life she was going to leave behind. It frustrated her. Playing the tough girl was wearing her down like a stone being eroded by rushing waves upon a shore. In her anger she cried out to God.

Lord God, I didn't think it would be this hard to say goodbye to everyone. The reality of it all seems so final. I'm feeling sad in my heart. Not as much for myself but more for those I am leaving behind. That is not exactly true. I'm feeling a little sorry for myself, too. Some of these people don't know you, Jesus. I must admit that I am confused to receive this death sentence. I thought you sent me back to help others. It doesn't make sense to me. Then again, your ways are different from our ways. Your wisdom is higher than our foolish thoughts. Part of me is feeling angry tonight at you, God. Maybe it is because I don't understand the purpose in all this. I'm angry that I have to leave these people who I love behind. I'm angry that I have to die so young, before I have had a chance to really make this life count for something. God, will you give me understanding?
Like rushing water from a broken dam, her thoughts flooded into her mind. She reached for her journal on her nightstand and began to write down her prayer..

'Tis but the hour of my destined fate. Casteth out before Him want or need. To know His love, His grace, His mercy. The dawning day from sunrise to sunset, I search for one thread of faith for which my weary head may rest. O awaken my Spirit from this dungeon of despair. Set forth my soul in thy love and peace to exist to the one who shall care. The unwise fool of pity, that is what I am; a fool to rise, a fool to sit, a fool to wait all day long, a fool to breathe, or guess or question. Thou hast made this fool I am. Thou can transform and make me wise. Strip from this mortal being the foolish skin, which suffocates this bleeding flesh.

Thou art divine in power and mercy. In a blink of an eye, a thought, thy breath of life may be released. Refresh this tainted soul. Sprinkle thy healing mist upon this heart that lies so bare. Life's ocean is endless like eternity. Senseless are all pondering thoughts, like waves upon an ocean. They stir the sand along the beaches of a mind. Who can fathom it? Thou sayest, "BE STILL." Thou knowest my coming and my going. Thou knowest all things upon a troubled shore, for thou hast made the shore and all who build upon it. No wonder thou sayest, "Who can fathom the wisdom of God? The wisdom of men is but foolishness." One must trust in thy Eternal Promise. Cast off all self. Thou can give strength, courage and peace divine. Grant that I may understand thy wisdom.

Ripley gently placed a bookmark in the last page of the book of Job as she read Job's words to the Lord. Job 42:3–6, *"I know that you can do all things; no plan of yours can be thwarted. You asked, 'Who is this that obscures my counsel without knowledge?' Surely I spoke things I did not understand, things too wonderful for me to know. You said, 'Listen now, and I will speak; I will question you and you shall answer me.' My ears have heard of you but now my eyes have seen you. Therefore I despise myself, and repent in dust and ashes."* (NIV)

25
Don't Pretend With Me

Ripley stayed with her mother for two weeks after telling her the news. Ms. Wilks was always an emotionally strong woman. Ripley's sister Lauren also wanted to spend some time with her. They didn't want her to go back to Kelowna, but when she explained the reasoning they understood and wanted to grant Ripley her dying wishes. Their conversations were rational and matter of fact. That in itself was a miracle in their relationships. They never used to agree on anything. Ms. Wilks and Lauren's request was that they phone each other often and that they would be notified of any changes in her condition.

The truth was, Ripley was already feeling the effects of the tumour. The intensity of the headaches at times made her sick. She was taking the painkillers more often than anyone knew. That is the way she wanted it to be. Abby picked her up to take her back to the brownstone, where they would pack for Ripley's trip back to the farm. Ripley couldn't get out of the house quickly enough, the pain was so bad. She didn't want them to see her in pain. The teary goodbyes took their toll on her physically. Lauren cried, saying goodbye, knowing it may be the last time she would see her. Ms. Wilks helped Abby get Ripley into the van. Ripley watched in the rear-view mirror, seeing her mother crying as she stood in the doorway waving goodbye. In fact, Ripley had never seen her mother cry before that day.

The ride was quiet. Ripley wasn't saying a word. She was just holding her head in her hands. Abby could see that something wasn't right and asked Ripley if she was okay. Ripley responded sharply, "I'm fine, damn it."

"No, you are not fine. You are in a lot of pain. Ripley, if you want me to help you, don't pretend with me."

"I'll be fine," Ripley said, almost ready to vomit. "Okay, I'm not fine, get me a bag and make it quick."

Abby pulled the van over to the side of the road and gave Ripley a bag. Ripley wanted to get home fast. All she wanted to do was go to bed.

Ripley had a bad couple of days, and was in no condition for a long drive to Kelowna. Abby had to call Roseway and tell her that they wouldn't be coming that week. Ripley told her to tell her that she had a bad case of the flu and she didn't want to go there and pass the flu around.

26
A Cup of Tea

Camay had not finished the book she had started writing back in the autumn, and was still working on it. This day, she just couldn't concentrate. Her source of information for this book had gone on vacation. It seemed like as good a time as any to go visit Roseway. Things still felt a little awkward between them because of what had happened. In fact, Camay saw Joseph more than she saw Roseway, which was somewhat unusual, considering Samson was her son. He respected Camay's motherly advice. He didn't blame her for her son's choices. Camay felt she had to make amends for Samson.

Camay baked a banana bread to take with her. It was a small peace offering. Walking up the front steps to the farmhouse, she watched the door fling open. Roseway greeted Camay with a bright smile and invited her in. "I saw you coming down the driveway. It is a lovely day for a walk, isn't it?"

Roseway was in a good mood, expecting that Ripley would soon be returning from her visit to Prince George. Camay replied, "Yes, it sure is. How have you been keeping? I see you have put on a little extra weight."

I'm feeling pretty good. The morning sickness has subdued. Thank God. I'm almost five months along. There are only four more months to go until this little bundle of joy is born."

Camay counted on her fingers. "So the baby was conceived in January."

"Camay, allow me to relieve any questions you may have. The baby is definitely Joseph's."

"How can you be so sure? Did you have a blood test taken?"

"No, we don't need to do that. We believe it to be so. Joseph and I are going to raise this baby as if it were his child."

Camay spoke with a tone of uncertainty in her voice. "I wish I could be so at ease about the paternity of the baby. I just wanted to put my mind at ease. Your answer doesn't really do that for me. However, I don't want what happened to be an issue of contention between us. You are a lovely young lady. It is easy to see how Samson could have taken a liking to you. It happened, and now let us put it all behind us. It is just as well you are taking that stand. Samson has a girlfriend now. I haven't met her yet. I'll be going to Ontario in August to visit the kids again. I was talking to Joseph and he mentioned that your friend Ripley is coming back to stay with you until the baby is born. She is a lovely girl. I only met her the one time."

"Yes, she is wonderful. I expect that she will be back sometime this week. Originally, she just went for a two-week visit. Then she decided to visit with her mother for a couple of weeks. She said she had a lot of loose ends to tie up before she moved here. The couple of weeks turned into a month. She will be here until the baby is born, and then she is getting a place in town by the hospital."

"I'm happy for you. Things seem to be much better for you now."

"Yes, we seem to be coping with everything." Roseway paused, trying to muster up a few more words. They seemed to get stuck on her tongue. "I just feel I should apologize for what happened. It was a huge mistake for both of us. Samson was no more to blame than I was. It just seemed to escalate out of control. I regret that it happened. I'm glad Samson has moved on, that he has a girlfriend. We all have to move on with our lives and learn from our mistakes along the way."

"I couldn't agree more. How about you make us a cup of tea to go with this banana bread?"

The phone rang while Roseway was pouring the tea for Camay. She put down the pot of tea while she went to answer the phone. "Hello."

Abby introduced herself over the phone. "Hello, is this Rose?"

"The name is Roseway. How can I help you?"

"My name is Abby. I'm a friend of Ripley's?"

"Is Ripley okay? Is there something wrong?" Roseway was somewhat short and to the point, fearing that something was wrong with her best friend.

"Yes, Ripley is very sick with the flu, and she asked me to call you to let you know that she won't be able to make it back to the farm this week like she had thought."

"Is she so sick that she can't phone me herself?" Rose was wondering why she had to hear the news from Abby.

"Actually, yes, she is. She said she would call you as soon as she stops vomiting. I think she was trying to be funny when she said that. Seriously, she really couldn't make the drive. Hopefully, she will be feeling better by next week. I'm sure she will give you a call in a day or two. She just didn't want you expecting her to arrive."

Roseway's mood took a hundred degree drop, feeling very disappointed. Lowly, she said, "Thank you for letting me know. Tell her I send my love. I hope she is feeling better soon."

"I will tell her for you. Sorry to be the bearer of bad news. When she is feeling better, I'll drive her down. Would you mind if I stayed at your place for a few days while I look around for a place in town? Ripley mentioned that you have quite a few rooms in your farmhouse."

"Well, yes, I suppose that would be fine. It is the least we could do for you. It is such a long drive to get here."

"It is not a bother to me. I would do anything for Ripley."

"So would I. We will hopefully see the two of you next week."

They hung up. Rose continued to pour the tea. The cup overflowed. Camay had already filled the cup, and Roseway hadn't noticed. She was so distracted by the conversation.

"Is there something wrong?" Camay asked.

Roseway sighed. "Well, that was Ripley's friend Abby. She told me Ripley is sick and they are not coming down now until next week. That friend of hers is starting to bug me."

"Roseway, I think it is called jealousy. Does it bother you that Abby is spending more time with Ripley than you are these days? You are feeling a little left out."

"Yes, that is exactly how I feel."

"Honey, jealousy is a big green monster. It just causes trouble. Nip it in the bud and everyone will be happier for it. Ripley is not well, so why don't we pray for her to get better soon, so she can visit?" Camay placed her hand on Roseway's and started to pray, *"Dear Lord, we ask that you put your healing hand on Ripley and give her a quick recovery from this flu. We pray that they will be able to come next week. Grant them travelling mercies, we pray. Help Roseway with these feelings of jealousy that seem to be bothering her. We give you thanks. Amen."*

27
The Secret

The headaches subsided after a few days. They had taken a lot out of Ripley. Her eyes looked drawn, and she had lost some weight with the vomiting. However, she was never more determined to do something.

With their bags packed, they drove the ten-hour trip, talking all the way there. They had some important plans to agree on before they arrived.

After hours of small talk, Ripley started the serious conversation. "This part of the journey may be difficult. Now I know what Acacia meant when she told me that I would have difficulties. It is obvious to you and me that this tumour is unpredictable. I can only control the headaches to a point, and then we know what happens. There will be other side effects that sneak up on us also. My friend, we have to be ready."

"What do mean?" Abby asked, apprehensive.

"I'm going to need you to cover for me from time to time. I have to keep this illness quiet until Roseway has the baby."

"You really think that Roseway is *that* fragile? Come on. I would want to know."

"Listen, you don't know Roseway the way I know her. Even when she does find out, I know that she will need help coping. She is having a baby. I don't want to see her digress from the progress she has been making. Their well-being is the most important thing to me right now. It actually helps motivate me to fight this tumour with all that I have. Knowing that, I need your help."

"Okay, I'll help you keep it under wraps as long as possible. But if I see that it jeopardizes your life, I'm out."

"That is reasonable enough. Now let's not talk about it anymore. There is Roseway's house."

Roseway bolted through the door and ran down the driveway holding her belly. Ripley put her window down while Rose walked along side of the van. Ripley's face lit up just seeing Rose's excitement. She always loved that childlike excitement that exuded from her. It made her feel alive, too. "Well kiddo, look at you. My, how you have grown since I last saw you. Sorry it took so long for me to get back. It was a nasty flu bug."

"That is okay. I'm just so happy that you are here now. I missed you." Roseway looked through the window. "Hello, you must be Abby. Welcome. Let's get you girls settled in."

Joseph was home, taking a couple days off between trips. They all sat down to a nice home-cooked meal. While they conversed over dinner, Joseph asked Abby about her music. He was quite impressed with the ministry the two girls had with their music. Joseph admired Christians who went out on a limb or put it on the line for the Lord. He drove truck for Transport for Christ, but never felt that he had enough opportunities to share his faith with others—at least not to the extent that he would like to.

Joseph asked if the two girls could sing a song acappella, because they had no instruments. They sang *Amazing Grace*. Their harmonies blended together like a bouquet of flowers. Leaning back on his wooden chair, Joseph listened attentively with his eyes closed, enjoying the sound. He thought they sounded like angels.

Ripley thanked him for the compliment, but interjected that she had heard angels sing, and words couldn't describe the awesome sound of their worship. They sang another song. Then Rose joined in singing with them. However, her voice was untrained and very much off-key. Joseph immediately opened his eyes to see what the horrible sound was that made him want to cringe. Roseway was singing with her eyes closed. She thought she sounded angelic, too, and she was singing with love and praise in her heart. The other three were so distracted that they looked at each other. The song ended. They couldn't help but smile.

Roseway asked Joseph, "What did you think of my singing? Did I sound like an angel, too?"

Ripley came to Joseph's rescue. "Why yes, Rose, you did. Did you know that the angels all have different kinds of voices? I would imagine that you sounded like an angel. God loves to hear us sing songs of praise. He doesn't care what it sounds like in the natural. It is the song of the heart that he hears."

Rose was enjoying singing so much that she pleaded, "That was fun, let's all sing another song."

Ripley answered, "How about a lullaby? I'm beat. It was a long drive. I don't mean to be a party pooper, but I think I'm going to go off to bed."

Joseph told them to go ahead. "You both must be exhausted from that drive. You do look very tired, Ripley. If there is anything you need, just let us know. I guess you are settled into your rooms? Don't worry about the dishes, Roseway and I will clean up this mess."

Abby asked, "Are you sure that I can't help?"

Joseph reassured her it was quite alright. The two girls went to their rooms. Roseway lit into Joseph. "Thanks a lot. You don't think I'm tired? I worked all afternoon cooking this dinner. I'm six months pregnant. Abby could have helped."

"I'm sorry, honey. I tell you what, I'll do the dishes and you can relax."

"You are very kind, Joseph. I'll help you. I shouldn't behave so miserably. I don't know what gets into me sometimes."

"Honey, you are pregnant and your hormones are probably doing push-ups. Your body is coping with many changes. The baby is growing, you are tired. I think it is normal."

"I'll be glad when this baby arrives and I can get my body back to normal."

"Rose, you look as beautiful as ever."

The days quickly turned into weeks. Abby was getting on Roseway's nerves. It seemed like Abby was always near Ripley. They were always whispering. It bothered Roseway that she couldn't have more one-on-one time with Ripley. She mentioned this to Ripley. "My, how time goes by. I just realized it has been two weeks since you both arrived here. I thought Abby was only going to stay here a few days?"

Ripley didn't know what to say to her. "Yes, I thought she would find a place by now. Did you know she sold her house and it closes at the end of August? The plan was that she go house-hunting for us while staying here."

Roseway tried to clarify. "I don't mind her staying here, but honestly, I just feel a bit like a third wheel in my own house. She won't leave your side for moment. You and I hardly get any time to talk. I think this is the first time since you've been here."

"Oh, really? I'm sorry. I didn't realize that we were excluding you. I don't think Abby was planning on staying much longer anyway."

Roseway didn't want to say much more, so she added, "I was just wondering, that is all."

Ripley talked to Abby about what Roseway had said. Ripley suggested that it might be better if Abby left for a month.

"I'll be fine, Abby. For the most part I haven't felt too bad. Besides, in a way it might be good for Roseway and me to have some time. I could use that time to help prepare her."

"How are you going to do that?" Abby asked.

"I'm not sure at the moment. I'm depending on God to help both of us. If things take a turn for the worse, then I'll call you right away. I'm sure God will let us know the right time to tell Rose. I'm counting on it. Keep praying that the Holy Spirit directs us."

Abby stayed for a couple more days, and reluctantly headed back to Prince George. While in Prince George, she would have an agent look for a place for her to live in Kelowna. The decision felt right within her spirit, even though she didn't know how long she would live there.

28
Sharing Life

It was a summer made for the vineyards. The many vineyards that weaved throughout the Kelowna area offered a beautiful panoramic picture. The surrounding mountains looked majestic, covered with tall pine trees. Ripley had always dreamed of taking a trail ride through the vineyards. The idea seemed crazy to Roseway when Ripley first mentioned it. She was worried about Ripley falling off the horse. Ripley had no fear.

They found a ranch that offered trail rides. The difficult part was getting Ripley on the horse. Ripley rather enjoyed having two strong, handsome ranch hands lift her up onto the horse. They strapped her legs into the stirrups and harnessed her to the saddle, so she wouldn't fall off. Roseway just laughed hysterically, watching. Then it was her turn to get on a horse. She couldn't lift her leg high enough because her stomach was quite the size. Roseway didn't think it was quite as funny, but the ranch hands gently lifted her onto the horse.

Her doctor had said an easy ride would not hurt the baby, but definitely no galloping. The horses followed the guide like they had ridden the trail a thousand times. They walked slowly through the vineyard. The guide did all of the talking while Ripley and Roseway just looked around at all the beauty of God's creation. They just drank it in like a fine wine while praising God. It was an amazing, spiritual experience that left them both overjoyed. Ripley thanked Roseway for being such a good sport and sharing with her one of the most awesome experiences she ever had.

The month went by quickly. Roseway said to Ripley that there was something that she always wanted to do but just never did it. She wanted to go on a hot air balloon ride. They planned a day trip. Ripley was hesitant at the idea. She was afraid of heights. Roseway encouraged her to conquer that fear. Ripley wouldn't turn down a challenge.

Up they went in the most colourful of balloons—bright orange, blue and yellow. As the balloon lifted off the ground, Roseway laughed with excitement, while Ripley clenched her teeth holding onto the railing with a white-knuckled grip. Roseway told Ripley not to look down, but out. It was the closest thing on earth to heavenly bliss. Ripley relaxed at the thought. They both just breathed in the cool air looking wide-eyed at the scenery. Ripley commented, "Just amazing."

"It sure is. When you look out from this perspective, it really shows you how small we are in comparison to everything around us."

"Yes, and it also shows how big God is. He created it all."

"The wind could pick this balloon up and just blow us into space. We would be gone."

"Interesting thought, Rose. Life can also be like that sometimes. We can be here one moment and gone the next." Ripley paused. "I have a question for you. Are you afraid of dying?"

"Well, I didn't think I was afraid of dying until you shot me with the gun that time. At that moment, all I could think was 'I want to live. I don't want to die.'"

Ripley thought about Rose's answer. "Were you afraid when you cut your wrists?"

A look of embarrassment clouded Rose's face. "Well, I wasn't thinking straight. At that moment I felt so ashamed of myself, and that overwhelming feeling almost seemed worse than death. Now, when I think about it, I'm more afraid of death itself, taking that last earthly breath. What about you, Ripley, are you afraid of dying?"

"No, I'm not afraid. We are all going to die one day. Some die sooner than others. I know what you mean about wanting to live, though. We think of living as breathing, smelling, touching and enjoying ours lives and the people who are in our lives. Rose, I have to tell you that when I was in that coma, I experienced something beyond this life here. If that experience is any indication of what it will be like to die, then when my time comes, I will welcome it.

"I think it is human instinct to fight against the unknown. For example, that baby you are carrying inside your womb is probably quite happy to stay there. It is comfortable, warm and secure. When the time comes for the baby to be born, Rose, you will experience the pain of childbirth and that little baby will fight to be born into this world. It really doesn't want to leave that safe place to come here. The baby will be born and find that there is a lot of love waiting for him or her. I think dying is the same. There is so much love waiting for us when we get to heaven. It is something that one has to experience to understand. It is different than the love here on earth. We love what we know. There is so much of God that we do not know. I think when we die here on earth, really we are coming alive in a new life with God. Waiting to go to that place that Jesus is preparing for us is like waiting for the best trip ever. The only drawback is for the loved ones we leave behind."

"Ripley, you paint a nice picture of death, but looking out from this hot air balloon makes me wonder, what could be any better than this?"

The change in altitude of the balloon was giving Ripley pain in her ears. Holding her head, she said, "We will see, Rose. Someday we will know what it is like."

The next morning, Ripley stayed in bed. The headache was causing her so much pain that she had taken an extra painkiller when she went to bed. She slept through breakfast. When lunch-time came around, Joseph went up and knocked on the door to see if Ripley was coming for lunch. When he knocked, he heard her vomiting. He asked her if she was okay. Ripley responded that she was fine. She washed her face in the basin that was beside her bed, but it didn't take away her pale complexion. Her head was pounding like tribal drums. Joseph put his head to the door to listen. He heard Ripley crying in prayer, "Oh God, please take away this pain. I would really love to live to see Rose's baby. This pain in my head is almost more than I can bear. I need your strength. Lord God, I know you can heal me with one touch of your hand. Let your will be done."

Joseph knocked, then opened the door, startling Ripley.

"Oh my goodness, you startled me."

"Sorry, I didn't mean to scare you. I wanted to see if you are feeling okay. Forgive me for eavesdropping, but I heard you praying. What is going on? Does Roseway know how sick you are? You look terrible. Do I need to call an ambulance?"

"Oh Joseph, I'll be fine in a day or two. Rose doesn't know anything about my sickness. I'm not telling her, either."

"How can you keep a secret like this from her? She should know."

"Listen to me, Joseph; I don't need this right now. I feel like the top of my head is going to erupt at any moment. I don't want to talk about it right now. Please, please understand. Please just tell Roseway that I am sick today. I'm staying in bed. Could you do something for me? Could you call the hospital and tell them that I won't be in to work today? The other thing you could do is empty this bucket, and may I trouble you to bring me a pitcher of water? Sometimes these attacks can last a couple of days. Please don't say anything else to Roseway, other than I'm sick. I will tell her when the time is right."

Joseph helped her back to her bed and retrieved the items that she had asked him to get. He told Roseway that Ripley was very sick and would be staying in her room all day. Roseway checked in on her a couple times throughout the day. Each time, she was sleeping. Ripley was pretty out of it with the painkillers.

By the third day, Ripley was feeling a little better. She didn't know if it was just because she had been taking so many painkillers. Roseway was concerned about Ripley. She didn't look well at all. Ripley was determined to get herself out of that bed and bite the bullet even if it killed her. Roseway prodded Ripley with questions of concern. "Have you visited a doctor since you have been here? You never did tell me how those tests turned out."

"Actually, I did visit Doctor West just last week after one of my shifts."

"What did he say?"

Ripley paused. *Should I tell her the truth? Joseph is right, I should tell her. I am getting worse. It could happen any day. I can't expect other people to lie about my condition. My mother and sister want to come down this Labour Day weekend. And I need Abby's help.*

Rose shook Ripley out of her daze. "I asked you, what did the doctor say?"

Ripley looked down at the floor, then up to the ceiling and back to the floor. She sighed.

Roseway was getting impatient and worried. She put her little hand under Ripley's chin and lifted her head. "Why aren't you answering me?" She asked with a concerned expression.

Ripley looked into Rose's eyes like they were deep, long tunnels. Ripley's eyes started to burn and redden as she fought the well of tears building up. It was difficult to say the words. It was like they were wrapped around her tongue. She could barely make a whisper as her throat tightened. "I ... am ... dying ..." Tears burst from her eyes like never before.

Roseway raised her voice. "Stop it. Can't be ... You can't die. We are best friends forever."

"I am dying. There is nothing the doctors can do. The only thing that will never change is what you just said, 'We are best friends forever.' Forever is a long time, Rose. Remember the hot air balloon ride. I'm just going on a vacation. Someday you will meet me there."

Roseway scrunched up her face, not wanting to accept the truth. "How long have you known?"

"Does it really matter?"

"You have known since you have been here, haven't you? That is what all the whispering was about between you and Abby. She knows about this. How could you keep this from me?" There was a pause of silence between them. Rose didn't want to accept the finality of those words. "Why don't you get a second opinion from another doctor?"

"Rose, both Doctor West and Doctor Spandecker have conferred with each other."

Angry, Rose said, "God always takes away the things that I love."

"Don't even go to that place. You are far beyond going back to that place of pity. It is not God's fault. I would be so sad if you turned away from God. Rose, you are the reason I have peace about dying. If I had never met you, I never would have come to know Jesus. It was your faith that made me call out to God that day. My life, my perspective and my attitude are just a few of the things that have changed in my life since meeting you and since accepting Christ.

"God brought you into my life for a reason. There is a purpose in all things. Sometimes we never find out what that purpose is. It would seem that He also brought me into your life for a reason. He will take me out, and someone else will come into your life and be your friend. It is all part of our journey. I thank God every day for bringing you into my life.

"So Rose, I know it will be very difficult initially when I'm gone. You will have a baby to love, for me. You have a husband to love. I will never have either of those things. There are many things I won't get to enjoy here. I will enjoy other things in heaven. This past summer and the time we spent together was so much fun. Why, we lived out two of our dreams, praise God. I only have one other dream to fulfill before I go. That dream is to hold your little baby in my arms. I never got to hold my own babies. I only have one request." She paused. "Pass me a tissue." She wiped her eyes and blew her nose. "Darn it, the secret is out. Now you know, deep down I am really a mush ball. I bet my face is all blotchy like yours."

Roseway couldn't help but laugh, because Ripley's face was all blotchy. "That was your one request, a tissue?"

"No!" Ripley laughed, too.

"Well, what is your one request?"

"That you name the baby after me."

Rose scrunched her face again. "Name her or him Ripley?"

"No, give them my real name."

Roseway forced a smile. "You are finally going tell me your real name?"

"Sure, why not. My real name is Agnus Wilks."

Roseway couldn't believe it. "No way...No wonder you changed your name to Ripley." Roseway just laughed out loud, then with a startled expression she groaned, "Oh, aww, the baby just did a summersault." Roseway grabbed Ripley's hand and put it on her stomach.

Ripley commented, "I think this kid is going to be a football player."

The baby moved within the womb again, then water gushed down Roseway's leg. Roseway didn't know what just happened. "I think I just pissed my pants."

"No Rose, your water just broke. You are going into labour."

"I'm in labour? The baby is three weeks early. I guess you are going to get your wish, Ripley. Where is Joseph?" Raising her voice, she yelled, "Joseph ... honey, get the truck ... now! We are going to have a baby!"

It was a family affair. Joseph rushed around the house in a panic. He grabbed a suitcase and quickly filled it with some clothes. Then he helped Roseway into the truck and lifted Ripley beside her. Ripley helped coach Roseway through the contractions by showing her how to breathe in a way which helped her cope with the pain. Ripley wasn't going to miss this birth. She had hoped to see this birth for months. Noreen rushed to the hospital to meet them when they arrived.

Fourteen hours of labour was enough for Roseway, and more than enough for Joseph. Rose gave birth to a gorgeous baby boy with a full head of black hair who looked just like Joseph. Rose and Joseph agreed that they would name their son Riley David.

Noreen looked like a proud grandmother. They put Riley in Roseway's arms and let him latch on to his mother. Rose just cried, looking at the little baby in her arms. Mom, isn't he just perfect? He looks like you, Joseph."

Ripley sat in her wheelchair, smiling as she watched the three of them already so in love with this newborn baby. She thought to herself, *God, there is a comfort in death and in life that can only come from you. Thank you for giving me the opportunity to be part of this momentous occasion.*

Joseph and Rose both looked at each other and then at the baby. Rose handed Riley to Joseph, and he walked over to Ripley and gently put the baby in her arms. She cuddled her arms around baby Riley and kissed him on the cheek. "How you doing, little guy? Welcome to this big new world. Here is a little gift from your Aunt Ripley. It is just a book, but it has a great story. It is about a little boy named David and a big giant named Goliath. Mommy and Daddy will have to read you the story for me. God Bless you, little Riley David."

29
The Sleep

Joseph and Roseway took Riley home after a couple of weeks. Doctors wanted the baby to put on a little weight before he went home. Abby settled into a nice little bungalow near the hospital, and Ripley moved in with Abby not long after the baby was born. Ripley continued to work with patients at the hospital three days a week. It would depend on the severity of the headaches. They became more frequent as time went on. Ripley was tough and stubborn and fought them with everything she had in her.

Joseph and Roseway celebrated their first anniversary in Hawaii. They wanted little Riley to see the world. Their love for one another was unbreakable. So many changes in their lives took place in that first year of marriage. They had both matured in many ways.

After the long overdue honeymoon, Roseway was expecting again. Ripley was still alive a full year to the day since she had stood in Doctor Spandecker's office while he read her the death sentence. Ripley would say that she lived a lifetime in that year, because she lived each day like it was her last. God had granted her many wishes. Ms. Wilks and Lauren visited that same week. They saw Ripley happy and alert, and opinionated as always. It was a blessing no one saw Ripley suffer. Sure, she had headaches. She became good at hiding her pain, the brave soldier she was. In fact, on that fateful night, Joseph, Abby, Roseway and Riley went to a Good Friday Service at the local church with Ripley.

That night, Ripley said her goodnights to all. For some reason, she had never liked to say goodbye. It seemed too permanent. When she hugged Roseway, she said, "See you, pal."

Roseway would always reply, "See ya."

Abby helped Ripley into her bed that night. Ripley said to her, "I'm really going to miss you and Rose when I'm gone. I hope the two of you will become best friends to one another. You are both my best friends forever. I love you both."

"Well, Ripley, we both love you, too."

When Ripley went to sleep that night, she would not awaken the next morning to the same life. She went into such a deep sleep that a darkness washed over her. Images of her life's snapshots began playing in her mind. It was like a wonderful dream. First she was in her mother's womb and felt the love and comfort of being there. Then she was just a little toddler taking her first steps into her mother's arms. She saw herself playing at the park with Lauren. Snapshots flashed of fun times with Roseway, walking the boardwalk along the Fraser River in Prince George, the hot air balloon ride, JD teaching her in psychology class, singing at the piano with Abby. Then the images faded like a movie coming to an end, and everything faded into dark.

She heard the heavenly sounds of violins playing in the distance. Acacia was quietly singing and playing her harp. A choir of angels also started to sing along. It was the biggest heavenly symphony that had ever assembled. They were all singing, "Come as you are. Come to me, my child, and I will give you rest. Come lay your burdens at my feet. Entrust yourself into my care. Come receive Christ the King. Come and live forever."

The voices were calling her home. The love she felt was drawing her to go. It was a love so strong, so amazing. The darkness began to disappear as she walked toward the sounds. Before her was a gate of many coloured gems: sapphires, emeralds, amethysts, diamonds and gold. She could see the light shining so bright, it seeped through the gate. It lit up everything around it. The gate began to open, and there stood Jesus. The glory of the Lord shined like the sun. In total reverence to God, she dropped to her knees. Jesus took her by the hand and raised her to her feet. She looked at him with admiration. The clothes she was wearing were snow white. Not an imperfection on her body anywhere. The white gown flowed down to the ground all around her. She was adorned like a princess bride. The trumpets played as she entered through the gate. She walked down that golden road like a bride walking to the altar for the first time.

Looking to the side of the aisle where many people gathered, she saw her earthly father Amadeus standing there, smiling. She recognized him and he recognized her. His lips didn't move. He just smiled but she heard him say to her, "Thank you for forgiving me. Jesus forgave me, too."

There were many other people there and they were all cheering. A little boy stood out in the crowd; he looked to be about twelve. She heard him say, "My name is Adam. My mommy and I watched you on this television show when I was in the hospital. I was very sick. We said a prayer that night. Thank you for telling your story."

Suddenly, she stopped in her tracks as her eyes fixated on one man who stood in the crowd. He looked so familiar, yet he had changed in some way. Realizing who he was, she gasped. It was Big Joe. The scar he'd had on his face was gone. His eyes no longer had a look of evil in them. The glory of the Lord shone in his countenance.

He had been washed and changed by the blood of the Lamb. He didn't speak either, but Ripley heard him say, "Thank you for the guidance you gave to my daughter Roseway."

Continuing to walk with Jesus by her side, she noticed another woman amongst the crowd jumping up and down. "My name is Sarah. You were right, Ripley. You told me that someday I would be made whole again. I was crippled and deformed and couldn't move without pain. Now I am free from pain, free to run, free to jump and rejoice. Thank you for telling me about Jesus."

The procession seemed to go on for miles. There was one person after another thanking her. Ripley didn't remember many of them, but they knew her. For they were some of the many souls who accepted Christ because of the life Ripley lived. In some small way she had shown Jesus to them. Their lives were changed for eternity. It was a marvel to Ripley to know that her life on earth had made a difference to so many people. She hadn't thought she had done that much.

Nearing the end of the long road that led to the Holy of Holies, Jesus turned to Ripley and said, "Follow me."

Ripley watched him walk ahead of her. He entered the temple and Ripley followed. The angels started singing, "Holy, holy, holy is the Lord Almighty, the whole earth is full of his glory." The train of his robe filled the temple. The Lord walked up and sat on the throne, high and exalted. Ripley knelt before him. Above the Lord there were seraphs, each with six wings: with two wings they covered their faces, with two they covered their feet, and with two they were flying. Ripley didn't feel that she was worthy to enter into the Holy of Holies, knowing of all her past sins. The Lord spoke. His voice was strong like the sound of rolling thunder. He opened a book and scrolled down and read Ripley's name from the Book of Life. The Lord picked up a crown from the table that was in front of him and he turned it around in his hand, looking at the many gems. “This crown I hold in my hand is for you, Ripley. Well done, my good and faithful one.”

The joy she felt was indescribable, undeniable, for she had passed from death to life because of Jesus. Then one of the seraphs flew to her with a live coal in his hand, which he had taken from the altar. With one touch of the coal on her lips, the Lord had taken away her guilt and her sin was atoned for. The Lord said to Ripley, “Whom shall I send? And who will go for us?”

Ripley said, “Here I am, Lord. Send me!”

He said to Ripley, “Go and tell the people as did my prophet Isaiah, “Be ever hearing, but never understanding; be ever seeing, but never perceiving. As you, Ripley, have learned to hear with your ears and see with your eyes and understand with your heart, so go and teach others to do the same.”

Abby went into Ripley’s room the next morning. Ripley looked like a doll lying there, so deathly still, covered up with a warm blanket. Abby ran her finger down Ripley’s cold, pale face. She didn’t flinch, not even a twitch. Abby looked at her with a solemn stare. The separation she felt seemed like her heart was being ripped from her chest. A tear rolled down her cheek and fell to the floor like a drop of rain. This was a day she had dreaded for months. She didn’t want to let her go. The clock on the wall ticked and tocked loudly. For Abby it felt like time stood still as she sat remembering all the great times they had shared. It prolonged the grief she was already feeling. A desperate prayer formed on her lips.

Father God, I know all things belong to you. You are the creator of all things. Our lives here on earth also belong to you. God, you say in your word that we will see even greater things than the miracles Jesus performed. Humbly, Lord God, I ask that my eyes would see a great thing today. With all my heart and with all my faith, Lord, I come to you like a little child. One who is saddened to see my friend Ripley lying in a deathly sleep. I ask in the name of Your Son Jesus Christ that you would perform a miracle today and bring my friend back to life. God, I believe that you can raise Ripley from this sleep in the same way you raised Lazarus from the dead. May the world see once again your amazing power? I also know that she belongs to you. May Ripley be a living testimony to all you have done and all that you will do? I ask this in Jesus' name. Amen.

Ripley gasped with a deep breath like she was breathing for the first time. She sat up in bed. Startled, Abby jumped back with a scream. Her scream frightened Ripley, and she screamed.

Ripley was confused. "What are you screaming about? You scared the life out of me. I was having the most amazing dream. I thought I died and went to heaven. Next thing I know, I wake up and you are screaming."

Abby was amazed and could hardly speak. Stuttering, she tried to say, "You ... were d-d-d-dead. Now you are a...live. Praise the Lord!"

Ripley noticed that her legs moved under the covers. "I can feel my legs. I'm very much alive. God has answered the many prayers for me to be healed. Praise the Lord!" Ripley slid her legs across the bed. She placed her feet on the floor like it was her first time. Wiggling her toes on the soft carpet, she stood to her feet. Slowly, she moved her foot to take the first step, like it was a step of faith into a new life, a new walk for the Lord. Her arms lifted high, reaching heavenward to praise him as she slowly turned around. Joyful tears of amazement covered her cheeks as she looked at Abby with an angelic expression, telling her, "I'm healed. I can walk. I can feel my legs. I am whole again. Can you believe it? Abby, God is not finished with me yet! My eyes have seen a glimpse of eternity. The almighty God has truly brought me to life for a great and important purpose. I will serve him all the days of my life."

In that heavenly place, I saw all the people we have to minister to. There are many people out there who we have to tell about Jesus. We have to teach them to hear and see and understand that Jesus is real. There is hope for eternal life through him. We have a calling to minister for God the gospel truth so that many will come to life in Christ Jesus. I have an amazing testimony to tell. Praise the name of Jesus. Hallelujah! I am Ripley Wilks, and I have a story to tell. I have to call my mother, Lauren and Roseway. This is amazing."

Abby and Ripley danced around the room. They were both so overcome with the joy of the Lord that they just laughed and cried.

Abby proclaimed in agreement, "Yes, yes I believe. Faith is like taking that first step of the day, when we don't even question the ability to breathe, walk or speak. Faith is alive when we just do it."

Doctor West and Doctor Spandecker couldn't explain with any concrete diagnosis why Ripley had regained the feeling in her legs so suddenly. They speculated that possibly the steroid medications Ripley was taking actually shrunk the tumour. The headaches she was experiencing were possible side effects of the blood vessels in her brain contracting. These contractions may have caused pain because of the many nerve endings in her brain. Other than it being the effect of the medications, the doctors were baffled. Was it a Jesus miracle or a wrong diagnosis? There are times when science does not have the absolute explanation.

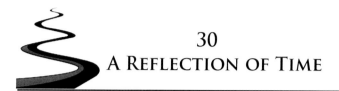

30
A Reflection of Time

Camay sat on her deck. The sun was shining on this bright summer day. She looked at her reflection on her laptop. *The image has changed somewhat,* she thought to herself. *Not quite as young and beautiful as I was twenty years ago. Oh, but here I am seventy years old now, finishing my next bestseller. Think positive, isn't that what Ripley always said? When I think of all the changes that have occurred over the past twenty years, I just shake my head. There are probably at least another twenty books with stories I could write. It takes time to write. When I think about God and all the life stories he has written, it boggles my mind. It shouldn't, because God is amazing. I never really knew just how amazing until I met Ripley Wilks. Her life testimony has touched millions of lives. I guess we never really find out just how many lives we touch in a lifetime. Do we touch their lives in meaningful ways or in bad ways?*

Ripley is still a powerful bible teacher and speaker at the annual Women of God Conferences where thousands of women gather each year. When she is not teaching or going on guest appearances, she is still working at the psychiatric unit in Kelowna.

John David Cleveland did come back into Ripley's life. They were engaged for two years. He transferred his teachings to the university in Kelowna when they married.

JD and Ripley enjoyed a wonderful outdoor June wedding at her mother's home in Prince George. Ms. Wilks spared no expense. Glass sculptures and extravagant gardens adorned the grounds of the backyard, which overlooked the Fraser River. Waiters dressed in black ties served the guests. A string quartet played music in the background. It was a perfect wedding day. Abby and Roseway were the bridesmaids, and Lauren was the maid of honour. JD had his best friend Mark and Joseph stand with him. Little Riley walked up the aisle bearing the rings on a little pillow.

Abby and Ripley continue to do special music together from time to time. Abby's music career really took off and she became a top-selling Christian artist. She finally got a music contract with Icon Records. It always bothered her to a point that God had not totally healed her legs. She learned to accept the limp and so did everyone else. It served as a reminder of the pain that she endured, and the pain others endure every day. It was constant motivation to get out there and help others with the word of the Lord.

Roseway and Joseph ended up having six children: Riley, Mathew, April, Daniel, Deborah and Rebekah. When they saved enough money, they eventually moved to the interior of British Columbia and built a house on the property where that old log cabin used to be. Roseway had inherited the land from her father Joe Demerse. Growing up there for many years, Roseway realized that she really did like the country lifestyle.

I don't see Roseway as much as I would like. The visits have become less frequent now that Noreen passed. That was sad. She had a bad bout with breast cancer. Doctors didn't find it in time. That was rough on Roseway, losing her mother. It is a good thing she has a husband like Joseph. He has always been such a devoted husband. Rose and Ripley write each other monthly, and visit whenever they can.

Roseway lost her naivety after having her first child, Riley. They raised their children in the ways of the Lord. There wasn't as much bad influence on the children, living in the mountains. They didn't have a television and they lived a very simple life. That is the way they liked it. Even so, they had their many trials and challenges to overcome, living where they were. Someday I'll tell you some more about that.

Abby, well, she never did find Mr. Right, at least not yet. She has a big measuring stick for that man to measure up to, whoever that man may be.

Here I am, finishing my last page, sitting on my porch at this old schoolhouse. The School of Zion is the name. My husband will be home soon. That is right, I also married a wonderful man and he will be home for his lunch soon. I better finish writing. Perhaps God has already written the last page of this book. Now on we go to the next.

Keep your eyes open, look with your eyes, hear with your ears and understand with your heart, read your bible and also keep a look out for the next book in *The Narrow Road* series: *Jenn – The Road of Sacrifice.*

DECISION

You can begin your new life in Jesus Christ today.My Decision to receive Christ Jesus as My Saviour.

Name:

Date:

I confess to you, God, that I am a sinner, and ask you, Jesus, to forgive my sins. I ask you to take total control of my life by becoming my Lord and personal Saviour. I ask you to walk with me always and lead me through all the days of my life. I believe that you are the Christ and that you died for my sins on the cross and that you were raised from the dead for my justification. I do now receive you and confess you, Jesus, as Saviour. Thank you for walking the road of sacrifice for me.

About the Author

With twenty years' writing experience, creative writing classes, and workshops, Rebecca compiled an anthology of her poetry called *Inspirational Poems of the Heart*. She has also recorded a CD of music titled Greater Love.

Rebecca's first book was published in 2005. *When Times Stands Still* is said to be like a moment in time for each of us to experience. It is a fresh, personal autobiography with a short chapter format with a bible study for each chapter. It was written under the pen name Rebecca Hickson and can be purchased on Amazon or through Xulon Press.

In five years, Rebecca's pen has been flowing. The anticipated arrival of The Narrow Road series is hot off the press. *Roseway—The Road that Never Ends* is the first book in the series. The sequel, *Ripley—The Road of Acceptance*, and the third book in the series, *Jenn—The Road of Sacrifice*, are riveting fiction novels covering a wide variety of modern-day topics.

Author's Artist Statement

In my writings I try to convey the message about the ultimate amazing love and hope we can have through Christ Jesus. My prayer is that all who read my writings will be encouraged to help others through their trials. In life sometimes we cry, sometimes we laugh, and once in a while we want to scream out loud. I believe that God hears our cries, even our most quiet whisper. Sometimes our trials can feel devastating. When all is said and done, God's plan is perfect. I write to inspire hope, faith, love and courage.

Website: rebecca-robinson.org